"You have your return ticket?" he asked, and she nodded. "Can I see it?"

Looking puzzled, she pulled a folded sheet of white paper from her fanny pack, which was almost hidden under the swell of her belly. Lucy handed him the sheet of paper and he promptly ripped it in half.

"Ookay," she said. "That was very dramatic and all. But you do realize that I can just print another one."

He crumpled the paper and tossed it into the backseat. "Call it a symbolic gesture."

"I got that part. I'm just not sure what it symbolizes."

"You're not going back to Florida."

She blinked in surprise. "I'm not?"

"You're going to stay here in Chicago."

"Where?"

"You're going to live with me. And as soon as we have time to arrange it, you're going to marry me."

* * *

Caroselli's Accidental Heir is part of
The Caroselli Inheritance trilogy: Ten million dollars
to produce an heir. The clock is ticking.

* * *

If you're on Twitter,
tell us what you think of Harlequin Desire!
#harlequindesire

Dear Reader,

There's nothing I love more than corresponding with my readers, and these letters are a golden opportunity for some "face time." A while back I started a "getting to know Michelle" series. Since Thanksgiving is only eleven days away as I write this, I think I will take it a step further, and call this the "Michelle's Holiday Tradition" letter.

As a family, we have many traditions, but these are two of my favorites. The first I like to call the Holiday Bait and Switch. This started with my husband's family. Instead of writing names on the gift tags of the kids' presents, each would receive a number, which would correspond with a child on my "master list" of gifts. So until Christmas morning, no one knew which gift belonged to which kid. This used to drive my kids crazy. It was awesome.

Another tradition, which started over twenty-five years ago and has carried on every year since, is painting Christmas ornaments and trinkets. Nothing fancy. Just the premade, unpainted kind you find at any craft store. Wood, plaster, glass. Whatever catches my eye. Shy of redecorating the house, it's the only time of year that I pick up a paint brush. When my daughter was old enough, she started to paint with me, and still does. Just the other day my granddaughter joined us, and we had three generations painting together. I hope that someday she will paint with her daughter, too.

So there you have it, a little bit more about Michelle. Maybe my next letter will be Michelle's most embarrassing moments....

Michelle

CAROSELLI'S ACCIDENTAL HEIR

MICHELLE CELMER

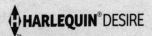

HARLEQUIN® DESIRE

Recycling programs
for this product may
not exist in your area.

ISBN-13: 978-0-373-73315-6

CAROSELLI'S ACCIDENTAL HEIR

Printed in U.S.A.

MICHELLE CELMER

is a bestselling author of more than thirty books. When she's not writing, she likes to spend time with her husband, kids, grandchildren and a menagerie of animals.

Michelle loves to hear from readers. Visit her website, www.michelecelmer.com, like her on Facebook or write her at P.O. Box 300, Clawson, MI 48017.

To Beppie, whose friendship means the world to me.

One

In twenty-three years, nine months and sixteen days, Lucy Bates had made her fair share of questionable choices. Due to her impulsive nature, her guileless curiosity—and an occasional lack of basic common sense—she'd found herself in more than a few...*complicated* situations. But her current predicament topped them all.

Note to self: The next time you have the bright idea to leave a man and move across country in the hopes that he'll follow you, don't bother.

Not only had Tony not followed her, he'd gone out and found someone new. After nearly a year of casually dating Lucy, and not a single mention of taking their relationship to the next level, he was marrying a virtual stranger.

Not only had he been dating this new woman a measly two months, *she* wasn't pregnant with his baby.

Lucy was.

She was a stereotype.

The poor girl who fell for the rich guy and got knocked up. And though there was a whole lot more to it than that, she knew that was all anyone would see. Including Tony.

"This is it," the cab driver announced as he pulled up to the house. Lucy peered out the window. Located in one of the oldest and most prestigious neighborhoods in Chicago, the Caroselli mansion put the neighboring homes to shame. It was old, and a little gaudy for her taste. But very grand.

The street was lined with luxury cars and SUVs, and children were playing in the park directly across the street. Tony once told her that his grandfather, the founder of Caroselli chocolate, liked to sit in his study, in his favorite chair, and watch the kids play. He said it reminded him of home. Home being Italy.

She handed the driver the last of her cash and climbed out of the cab. The sun was shining, but there was a chill in the air.

She'd blown her entire savings account on a roundtrip plane ticket from Florida to Chicago, paying the exorbitant Sunday rates, so from here on in she would have to rely on her credit card. If she maxed that out…well, she would think of something. She always did.

But it wasn't just about her anymore. She needed to start thinking like a mother, putting the baby first.

She laid a hand on her swollen belly, felt the thump thump of itty bitty feet against her palm, never so confused, or terrified, or content in her whole life.

She promised herself right then that if she could just figure this mess out, she would never do another impulsive thing for as long as she lived.

And this time she meant it.

"You've got him right where you want him," her mom had told her on the way to the airport that morning in her clunker of a car that always seemed to be one repair away from the junkyard. "Whatever he offers you to keep this quiet, you ask for double."

And that was her mom in a nutshell.

"I'm not looking for hush money," Lucy said. "I don't want anything from him. I just think he should know about the baby before he gets married."

"That's what the phone is for."

"I need to do this face-to-face." She owed him that much after the way she'd behaved. He didn't want Lucy, that much was obvious, but this was his baby, too. She had no right to keep this from him.

"By crashing his engagement party?"

"I am not crashing anything. I'm going to talk to him before the party."

What she hadn't counted on was her flight being two hours late, which gave her only about two hours to get to Tony then get back to the airport for her return flight. Now she had no choice but to talk to him at the party. But she had no intention of making a scene. With any luck, people would just assume that she was another guest. A friend of the bride perhaps.

All she needed was five minutes of his time, and then they could both get on with their lives. If he wanted to be a part of the baby's life, that would be wonderful. If he tossed a dollar or two her way every so often to help with expenses, she would be eternally grateful. If he didn't, if he wanted nothing to do with her and the baby, she would be disappointed, but she would understand. After all, hadn't she been the one to insist that they keep it casual? No obligations, no expectations. How could she then turn around and expect him to take responsibility for a child he never wanted?

Nope, nothing suspicious about that.

"Even if he wasn't engaged, baby or no baby, that man would never marry you," her mom had told her. "Men like that only keep women like us around for one reason."

A fact she loved to remind Lucy of every chance she got. And she was right. Lucy had told herself a million times that Tony was too good for her, that even if he did want to settle down someday, it would be with someone from his own side of the street. And that's exactly what he'd done.

She and Tony were from two very different worlds, and she had been a fool to ever believe that he would follow her to Florida and beg her to come back, to hope that he would miss her. All she could do now was try to pick up the pieces of the mess she had created. Which meant shelving her pride and accepting his financial help if he offered it.

Well, she thought, the mansion looming ahead of her, *it's now or never.*

Heart in her throat, and before she lost her nerve, Lucy rushed up to the front porch and knocked on the door. Her knees felt squishy and her heart was pounding, but after a minute or so no one answered, so she knocked again.

She waited, but still no answer.

She was already off to a rip-roaring start. Could the individual who sent her the email have been wrong about the date of the party? Or the time? Or even the location?

And what woman in her right mind would take the word of a typed letter from an anonymous "friend"?

This one would. And it was too late to turn back now.

She tried the knob and found it unlocked. Why not add breaking and entering to her list of transgressions?

She eased the front door open, peering inside. There was no one in sight, so she stepped in, snapping the door quietly closed behind her. The foyer and adjacent living room were elegantly decorated and showplace-perfect. And too quiet. Where the heck was everyone? Maybe it really was the wrong day, and the cars outside were for another house, and a different party.

She was about to turn around and slip back out the door when she heard faint music from the rear of the house. String instruments. Maybe a quartet? She couldn't make out the melody.

Thinking she might actually have a chance to slip into the party unnoticed, she followed the sound of the music, passing a spectacular dining room decorated in deep hues of red and gold with a table long enough to accommodate a small army.

The music stopped abruptly and she turned. Across from the dining room was an enormous family room with a stone fireplace that kissed the peak of a cathedral ceiling. Rows of chairs lined either side of a silk runner....

Oh. My. God.

This was no engagement party. It was a wedding!

What struck her immediately was the normalcy of it all. The tradition. The handful of wedding guests perched on satin-covered folding chairs. The bride with her long, elegant neck and blade-like cheekbones. Her dress, an off-white shift, was as simple as it was stylish, while showing off a pair of legs so slender and long, they brought her nearly to eye level with Tony, who at six feet two inches was in no way lacking height.

Speaking of Tony...

Lucy's heart lifted the instant she laid eyes on him, then slammed to the pit of her stomach. In a tailored suit, his jet-black hair combed back off his forehead, he looked as if he'd stepped off the cover of *GQ*, but in a mussed, I'm-too-sexy-for-my-shirt way. Very much the way he looked the first time she saw him in the bar where she'd worked. And until that very second she hadn't realized just how much she had missed him. How much she needed him. Until he came along last year, she never *needed* anyone.

So what now? Should she slide into one of the empty seats and pretend to belong there, then talk to him after the service? Or should she turn and run back out the door and phone him later, as her mom had suggested.

"Lucy?" Tony said.

She blinked out of her stupor and realized Tony was looking right back at her. And so was the bride. In fact, everyone in the room had turned and all eyes were fixed on her.

Oh, boy.

She stood there frozen, wondering what she should do. She'd come here to *talk* to Tony, not crash his wedding mid-ceremony. But she was already here, and the wedding was already disrupted, and running and hiding wasn't an option. Why not do what she came to do?

"I am so sorry," she said, as if an apology would mean diddly-squat at this point. After this, if he ever spoke to her again, it would be a miracle. "I didn't mean to interrupt."

"Yet here you are," Tony said, his tone flat. He once had told her that he admired her spunk, and the fact that she had the courage to speak her mind, to stand up for what she believed in, but she doubted this was what he'd had in mind. "What do you want?"

"I need to speak to you," Lucy said. "Privately."

"*Now?* If you hadn't noticed, I'm getting married."

Oh, she noticed.

The bride looked back and forth between the two of them, her face pale, as if she might faint. Or maybe she always looked that way. Come to think of it, she bore an uncanny resemblance to Morticia Adams. "Tony? Who is this?" she asked, her brow wrinkled in distaste as she looked down her nose at Lucy.

"No one of any consequence," he said, and did that ever sting. On the bright side, he would be eating those words very soon. Though that would hardly help to improve her situation.

"It's important," she told him.

"Anything you have to say to me, you can say right here," Tony told Lucy. "In front of my family."

Not a good idea. "Tony—"

"Right here," he insisted, pointing to the floor to make his point.

She recognized that rigid stance, the look of unwavering resolve. He wasn't going to back down.

If that was really what he wanted…

Head held high, shoulders squared, she unzipped her jacket, exposing the basketball-sized bump under her snug-fitting T-shirt, cringing inwardly as a collective gasp cut through the silence, reverberating off the velvet-covered walls. She would never be able to forget that sound, or the look on everyone's faces for the rest of her life. If Tony had been aiming to embarrass Lucy or humiliate her, it had backfired. The bride was the one who looked mortified.

"Is it yours?" she asked Tony, and he looked to Lucy questioningly. She shot him a look that said, *What do you think?*

He turned back to his fiancée and said, "Alice, I'm sorry, but I need a minute with my…with Lucy."

"I suspect it will take considerably longer than a minute," Alice said, her voice tight. She slipped the diamond engagement ring from a long, slender, claw-like finger and held it out to him. "And something tells me that I won't be needing this any longer."

"Alice—"

She stopped him. "When I agreed to marry you, a pregnant lover wasn't part of the deal. Let's just cut our losses, shall we? Keep it dignified."

Was that all their marriage was to Alice? A deal? She looked humiliated, and seriously annoyed, but heartbroken? Not so much. And maybe her fingers weren't so clawlike, Lucy thought as she watched Alice fiddling with the ring. Good thing, too, because she looked as if she'd like to gouge out Lucy's eyes.

Tony didn't try to change her mind. He obviously knew a lost cause when he saw one. Or maybe he didn't love her as much as he thought. Lucy couldn't help feeling that she had just done him a favor, though she doubted he would see it that way. He would probably never forgive her.

Alice tried to hand the ring to him, but he shook his head.

"Keep it," he said. "Think of it as my way of saying I'm sorry."

Considering the size of the rock, that had to be at least a five-figure apology. As consolation prizes went, Alice could have done a lot worse.

Alice palmed the ring, accepting her defeat with the utmost grace, and Lucy actually felt sorry for her. "I'll go get my things."

A woman in the front row whom Lucy recognized from pictures as Tony's mom, shot to her feet. Which, even in three-inch heels barely brought her to shoulder height with her ex-future-daughter-in-law.

"Alice, let me help you," she said, slipping an arm around hers and leading her from the room, shooting Lucy a look that said, *Just wait until I get my hands on you.* Despite being in her sixties, and no larger than

Lucy—sans the baby weight, of course—if she was anything like her son she would be a formidable adversary. And after what Lucy had done today, she couldn't imagine they would ever be anything but enemies.

One more stupid act to regret. Her relationship with her child's grandmother forever scarred before it even began. In Lucy's world this sort of thing happened all the time, but the Carosellis were cultured and sophisticated, and she knew now, way out of her league. How could she have ever believed that she and Tony could have a future together? Her mom was right. Men like him didn't marry women like her.

The instant Alice was out of sight the silence dissolved into whispers and murmurs. Lucy couldn't hear what any one person was saying, but she had a pretty good imagination.

It wasn't supposed to be like this.

A man she recognized as Tony's father stepped over to speak to him, taking Tony by the arm. Physically, two men couldn't have looked more different. Tony was long and lean and fit, while his dad was shorter and stocky. Other than their noses—which most of the Caroselli family seemed to share—they didn't look a thing alike.

After a few brief, but sharply spoken words, the elder Caroselli left in the direction his wife had gone, but not before he shot Lucy a look that seemed to say, *I'll deal with you later.*

Lucy felt so horrible already, nothing he could say or do could make matters worse than they already were.

Tony walked over to where she stood, his expression unreadable. But he looked so good her heart ached. She longed to wrap her arms around him and hold on for dear life.

You can't have him.

There was a point early in the relationship when his emotional unavailability had been his most appealing quality. She had stupidly believed that because she had never let herself fall in love, she was immune to the experience. And by the time she had figured out what was happening to her, it was too late. She loved him.

But on the very slim chance that he planned to pull her into his arms and profess his undying love for her, now would be the time.

He curled his fingers around her arm instead, and said in a tight voice, "Let's go."

She hesitated. "Go where?"

"Anywhere but here," he mumbled, glancing over at the guests who were now huddled in small groups and watching the action with brazen curiosity. Hadn't he told her a million times how nosy his family were, how he wished everyone would mind their own business? Could she have picked a worse place to do this?

Tony's grip was so firm, all Lucy could do was try to keep up with his much longer stride as he half walked/half dragged her to his car out front. But he was touching her, so she didn't even care. How pathetic was that?

He opened the passenger door for her, then he got in the driver's seat, but instead of starting the engine, he just sat there. She waited for the explosion. For Tony to accuse her of ruining his life. Then out of the blue, for no reason at all, he started to laugh.

Lucy was looking at him like he was nuts and she was probably right. Like some divine intervention, she had appeared just as he was about to make the absolute worst mistake of his entire life. And all he could think when he turned and saw her standing there was *Thank God I don't have to do this.*

"Are you all right?" Lucy asked him, looking as if she was seriously concerned for his mental health. And he couldn't blame her. Since she left he'd made nothing but misguided—and at times irrational—decisions. Like offering Alice a deal after only a month of dating. They didn't love each other, but she wanted a baby, and he needed a male heir. With a thirty-million-dollar inheritance riding on it, who could blame him for compromising? But he could see now what a mistake it would have been. Hell, he'd known it thirty seconds after he proposed.

All along, he'd kept reminding himself that the marriage need last only long enough to produce a male child. Then he and Alice would go their separate ways. But as the Wedding March had started to play, and he saw Alice walking toward him, he realized that not only did he not love her, he didn't really like her all that much, and even if they had to tolerate each other for only a year, that was a year too long. And if they did have a child, divorced or not, he would be shackled to her for the rest of his life.

Crisis averted thanks to Lucy. How was it that she always showed up when he needed her? She just seemed to *know*. And damn, had he needed her today. She was his voice of reason when he acted like a dumbass. And lately, especially since she had left, he'd risen to the level of king of the dumbasses.

Marry a stranger? What the hell had he been thinking?

He nodded toward her stomach. "Is this the reason you left?"

She bit her lip and nodded.

"I don't get it. Why didn't you just talk to me?"

She avoided his gaze, wringing her hands in her lap. "I'll be the first to admit that I handled this whole situation badly. I have no excuse for my behavior. And I'm not here because I want or need anything from you. And I definitely didn't come here to break up your wedding. That was just bad timing."

He thought it was pretty good timing, actually. "So why are you here? Why come back now?"

"I heard that you were getting married and I thought you should know about the baby before you did. But I had no idea you were getting married *today*. I was told it was an engagement party."

Which would explain her look of horrified shock when she realized what she had walked into. "Told by whom?"

"Does it really matter? I swear I didn't mean to cause any trouble. I just wanted to talk to you."

Lucy never went looking for trouble—hell, she didn't have a hurtful or vindictive bone in her body—yet somehow trouble always managed to find her. And though he had every right to be angry with her, furious even, she looked so remorseful, so beside herself, he just couldn't work up the steam. In fact, his first instinct when he'd seen her standing there, her jaw hanging open in surprise, had been to pull her into his arms and hold her. "So, talk to me. Why didn't you tell me about this sooner?"

"I know I should have," Lucy said, idly fiddling with the zipper on her jacket, avoiding his gaze. "I just…I didn't want to be *that* girl."

"What girl?"

"I didn't want you to think that I'd gotten myself knocked up on purpose, so you would feel obligated to take care of me. I'm not even sure how this happened. We were always so careful. At least, I thought we were."

Tony had learned a long time ago that in life there were no guarantees. All they could do now was make the best of a complicated situation. Getting rid of Alice was a decent start.

"First off, let's get one thing straight," he told her. "I do not, nor would I ever suspect you of doing anything so deceitful. I know you better than that. You just don't have it in you. And I'm sure you believed you were doing the right thing by leaving, but it was wrong to keep this from me."

"I know. I didn't think it through. I don't blame you for being angry."

"I'm not angry. I'm…disappointed."

She bit her lip and tears welled in her eyes, but she held them back. "I know. I screwed up. And I'm so sorry. I feel so bad for your fiancée."

"Alice will be okay." Tony had tried to convince himself that everyone was wrong about her, when deep down his gut was telling him that she would be a terrible wife, and an even worse parent. She was materialistic and demanding, and far too self-absorbed. She had a single favorite topic: Alice. She would go on for hours about the fashion industry and her fame as a runway model, and though he'd tried to feign interest, he often found himself tuning her out.

She had good qualities, too. She was attractive, if not a bit exotic-looking, had a decent sense of humor, and the sex had been okay, but they never really connected. Not the way he and Lucy had. From the first kiss, he knew Lucy was special. And she was adamant that she wasn't looking to settle down.

He was sure the right man for Alice was out there. It just wasn't him. They had a total lack of common interests. She liked the theater while he preferred a good shoot-'em-up action flick—the more action the better. She was a cat person and he was allergic. She was a vegan, he was a meat-and-potatoes man. She listened to New

Age hippie music and he jammed on Classic Rock. The louder the better.

Two people couldn't have been less compatible.

"Do you love her?" Lucy asked him.

He barely knew her. "Our relationship is…*was* complex."

He would like to believe that he would have stopped things before they went too far. Like when the priest asked if there was anyone who opposed the marriage. Or had he been hoping his family would do it for him? They had yet to warm to Alice, if that was even possible, and were vehemently against the marriage. Even *Nonno,* who had been trying to marry him off for years, and had gone so far as to bribe him with a thirty-million-dollar inheritance, refused to attend the wedding in protest.

"You should have trusted me," he told Lucy. "You should have told me the truth, and we could have worked something out."

"Like I said, I screwed up. I made a mistake. But I'm here now and I want to make things right."

Did she? Or would he come home one day a year or so from now and find her gone again?

Two

Tony had so many questions, and so many things he wanted to say to Lucy, he didn't know where to begin. It had been a shock to stop by her place all those months ago and be told by her roommate that Lucy had moved back to Florida with her mom. Lucy was such a private person, half the time he had no idea what had been going on in her head. Only now, sitting here beside her, did he appreciate how much he'd missed her, how much he had depended on their friendship. Since she'd left, he'd had no one to talk to. He'd long ago been labeled the strong silent type by his family. Serious, super-focused and private, but there was so much more to him that he didn't let people see. With her he could let down his guard and be himself. She was the only one who really *got* him.

Maybe that's why her leaving had been such a hard-hitting blow. It had been unsettling. He'd spent the better part of that last thirty years avoiding emotional entanglements.

Someone rapped on his window and Tony nearly jumped out of his skin. It was his cousin Nick. Christ. Couldn't he have ten minutes without *someone* in his family accosting him. He was guessing that Christine and Elana, his younger sisters, weren't far behind.

Tony rolled his window down. *"What?"*

Nick leaned down so he could see them both, resting his arms in the open window, looking first at Tony then Lucy. "Everything okay out here?"

"Lucy, you remember my cousin Nick," Tony said.

"Hi, Lucy," Nick said, shooting her a megawatt smile. "Let me be the first to congratulate you both."

Tony recognized the twinkle of curiosity in Nick's eye, and knew exactly what he was thinking. He was wondering if Tony was still going to take advantage of *Nonno*'s offer. Both Nick and Rob had forfeited their cut of the thirty million to save their relationships with their wives. But Tony had no marriage to save. Although to get the money he would have to marry Lucy. *Nonno*'s game, *Nonno*'s rules. But, if he could talk Lucy into marrying him, which in itself could be difficult, it wouldn't be a *real* marriage. She didn't want that.

"My wife is pregnant, too," Nick told Lucy. "We're due September twenty-first."

"Early June," Lucy said, and Tony could see Nick doing the math in his head. The slight tilt of his head and peak of his brow said he had come to the same conclusion as Tony—Lucy had known about the baby for quite some time before she left for Florida.

"I thought this was going to be a boring wedding," Nick said with a grin. "But this was even better than my sister's wedding, when my dad got into a fistfight with my mom's date."

A distinction Tony would be happy to forget.

"Is Alice all right?" he asked Nick, noting the pained look on Lucy's face. She really did seem to feel bad for Alice.

"She's still upstairs with your mom. Carrie is going to drive her back to the condo. She sent me out here to tell you to be gone before they leave."

Carrie was their cousin Rob's wife, and Alice's best friend. She had introduced Tony to Alice, a move she was probably regretting about now.

Alice being the polar opposite of Lucy had appealed to him. At first. In the end, it only worked against them. He often found himself wishing that she was Lucy, or at least a lot more like her. Those were two months of his life he would be happy to forget. Or erase completely. If it were within his power to go back in time and change things, he would have followed Lucy to Florida and convinced her to come back where he could take care of her. Where they could be a family, even if it wasn't in the traditional sense.

Hindsight was indeed twenty/twenty.

"Carrie also wants to know if Alice left any of her things at your place," Nick said.

"I don't think so, but I'll take a look around." Alice had only been to his town house a couple of times. Which made the fact that he was going to *marry* her all the crazier. Come to think of it, he wasn't even sure how old she was. He'd asked, but he'd gotten a vague nonanswer.

Dude, what the hell were you thinking?

"Do it soon," Nick said. "She's already talking about going back to New York in a couple of days."

"Permanently?"

"Far as I know."

Tony hadn't intended to drive her out of Illinois, but on the bright side, he wouldn't have to see her again. He could live with that.

The front door of *Nonno*'s house opened and people

started to file out onto the porch. Thankfully Alice wasn't among them. Nor were his sisters.

Tony turned to Lucy. "Why don't we go back to my place?"

She nodded, looking anxiously toward the front door.

"I'll talk to you later," he told Nick, who straightened up and made a "call me" gesture with his thumb and pinkie. The Carosellis were known for two things: chocolate and a propensity for gossip. To be honest, Tony'd had enough of both. He wanted out from under the microscope. He wanted the freedom to live his life however he wanted, both personally and professionally. To be who he wanted to be. Not what was best for the family, but what was best for *him*. It was what he'd wanted for a long time now. That thirty million dollars had been his ticket out. He could start over, build his own business. Be his own man.

But at what cost?

Tony started the engine and pulled away from the curb.

"That was…weird," Lucy said and he glanced over at her. He had to fight the urge to reach over and take her hand. He just wanted to touch her. But now didn't seem the time.

"What was weird?"

"After what I did, I figured your entire family would hate me."

It was much more likely that they would be planning to throw her a parade. His family hadn't exactly warmed to Alice. As in, none of them. He was pretty sure Rob liked her only because she was his wife's best friend. Just last night he overheard his sister Alana tell his mom that she thought Alice was a bloodsucking she-devil. "Let's not worry about my family," he told Lucy. "This has nothing to do with them. We need to talk about the baby. And about us."

"You're right."

He was glad she thought so, since he was winging it. He had never been in a situation like this. Nor did he know anyone who had. The true scope of how his life was about to change hadn't really sunk in yet, so he was still in a minor state of shock. Over what was to come, but also over what he had almost done today. Thankfully Lucy had been here to save him from himself.

"How has your pregnancy been going? You and the baby are both healthy?"

"I feel great, the baby is active and kicking just like he should be."

His heart skipped a beat. "He?"

She flattened her palms against her belly and the ghost of a smile tugged at the corners of her mouth. "Or she. I just have this strong feeling it's a boy."

That would be awfully convenient. "Where is your suitcase?"

"I didn't bring one. I wasn't planning on staying long. In fact…" She pulled her cell phone out of her jacket pocket and checked the display. "I have to get back to the airport soon. So we don't have a huge amount of time."

At first he thought she was joking. Did she honestly believe he was just going to let her leave again? While she was pregnant with his baby? He thought she knew him better than that. Of course, if she did, she wouldn't have left in the first place.

They may not have planned this, but as long as she was carrying his child, she was his responsibility, so for the time being, she was more or less stuck with him. And if the baby really was a boy, he would make his daddy a very wealthy man. If Lucy would marry him, that is.

It sounded simple enough; the only problem was that Lucy was as relationship-phobic as him. Probably even more so. She had been the one to set the boundaries of their relationship, to insist that they keep it casual. Now he had to figure out a way to convince her that getting married was best for the baby.

"You have your ticket?" he asked, and she nodded. "Can I see it?"

Looking puzzled, she pulled a folded sheet of white paper from her fanny pack, which was almost hidden under the swell of her belly. In all the time he'd known her she'd kept her belongings in either a beat-up backpack that she'd picked up in the lost and found at work, or a fanny pack. He'd never seen her carry a conventional purse. There was very little about Lucy that he would call conventional. She marched to the beat of her own drum.

Lucy handed him the sheet of paper and he promptly ripped it in half.

"Oooookay," she said. "That was very dramatic and all. But you do realize that I can just print another one."

He crumpled the paper and tossed it into the backseat. "Call it a symbolic gesture."

"I got that part. I'm just not sure what it symbolizes."

"You're not going back to Florida."

She blinked in surprise. "I'm not?"

"You're going to stay here in Chicago."

"Where? My roommate moved to Ohio. Not to mention that I don't have a job."

"You're going to live with me. And as soon as we have time to arrange it, you're going to marry me."

If that was Tony's idea of a marriage proposal, no wonder he was still single.

How many times had she fantasized about him asking her to marry him? This particular scenario was not at all what she'd had in mind. Technically, he hadn't even asked. He'd issued an order.

Could anything be less romantic?

"Why would I do that?" she asked, giving him the perfect opportunity to redeem himself.

"I know how against marriage you are," he said, "and I understand how you feel, but I really believe this is what's best for the baby."

Wrong answer, dude.

Not only did he drop the ball, he smashed it flat. He didn't even try to sugarcoat it. He would only be marrying her for the baby's sake. So much for those sentiments of love she'd been hoping for. Why didn't he just reach into her chest and rip out her still-beating heart?

Her mom would have jumped at the opportunity to have a rich and handsome guy take care of her, which is exactly why Lucy couldn't allow it. Though she couldn't deny it would be wildly entertaining to see her mom's expression when she heard the news.

"That sounds like a really bad idea," she told him, and the deep furrow between his brows said he disagreed.

"It's not," he said, as if he expected her to just take his word for it.

"If I marry you, it will confirm what everyone in that house was already thinking. That I got pregnant on purpose to trap you. That I'm looking for a meal ticket." Just the way her mom had with Lucy's father. What he had neglected to mention during their brief affair was that he was already married with a family. He had no interest in being a parent to his illegitimate daughter. He'd sent the obligatory monthly check, but when he died three years later, the gravy train—and any hope that he and Lucy might someday meet—died with him.

Lucy had three siblings she had never even spoken to, and whose lack of contact over the years said they had no interest in meeting their illegitimate half sister. She could only imagine what they must have thought of her. And her mother.

"I'll make sure everyone knows that isn't the case," Tony said.

If only it were that simple. "That never works. People are going to believe what they want to believe, regardless of what you tell them."

His deepening frown said he was getting frustrated with her. "Why does it even matter what my family thinks?"

It mattered to her. She loved Tony, and she wanted to be his wife, even knowing the rest of his family would probably never accept her. But not like this. Not because it was convenient. Or good for the baby. She wouldn't be anyone's consolation prize. "I can't marry you."

"Sure you can."

"No. I really can't.

"I want to take care of you." He took her hand and held it tight. "You and the baby."

She pulled her hand free. "Thanks, but I can take care of myself."

"If you won't marry me, would you agree to stay with me? At least until the baby is born?"

"I can't."

She could tell by his expression that he thought she was being stubborn, and maybe she was a little. But who could blame her? The dynamic was simple. She loved Tony, and he felt *obligated*. Living together would be painful enough. Marrying him would be downright torture. She could fool herself into believing that his feelings might change, but the reality was if he hadn't fallen in love with her by now, odds were good he never would. To marry him, even if it was for the baby's benefit, seemed sad and pathetic. She refused to play the victim.

Been there, done that, burned the T-shirt.

Maybe when they were alone at his place he would pull her into his arms and hold her tight, and tell her he was miserable and lonely after she left. Of course he would have a very logical, not to mention romantic, reason for not coming after her.

And maybe the Pope would convert.

Tony pulled down his street and found a spot close to his building. She'd been a little shocked the first time he brought her there. Everything about Tony screamed rich and classy. He drove a luxury import, drank the best scotch, owned a closet full of designer brand clothes, yet he lived in a nondescript apartment in an equally nondescript building, in what seemed to her to be one of the most boring streets in the entire city of Chicago. But as he had logically put it, why spend a lot of money on a place when he was hardly ever there?

Normally he would have held her hand as they walked into the building and got in the elevator. Often he even got frisky during the ride up, but this time he didn't touch her. She was both relieved and disappointed.

After a history of nomadic tendencies, Lucy had learned to never attach deep personal feelings to places, but when Tony unlocked the door and she stepped inside his apartment, she got a lump in her throat. She had so many good memories of the time they'd spent here together. At some point in their relationship his place had begun to feel like a second home to her, and she had fooled herself into thinking he might actually want her there with him.

Shame on her for forgetting who she really was.

Tony shut the door behind them and when he touched her shoulder her heart stopped. But then she realized that he was only helping her with her jacket, which he tossed over the back of the sofa. His suit jacket landed on top of it, and his tie on top of that. "Would you like something to drink? I have juice and diet soda. Or I could make tea."

"Just water," she said. There were newspapers strewn across the coffee table and a blue silk tie draped over the back of the leather chair. Guy furniture. The apartment was full of it. Leather, metal and glass. Bare wood floors. She would have thought that something might have changed in the four months she'd been gone, but everything looked exactly the same. And she saw no evidence of a woman staying there.

"Sit down," he said, gesturing to the sofa, more an order than a suggestion. He was working up to something, she could feel it. For every second he didn't speak, her nerves wound tighter as her hopes for a civilized solution faded. Responding to her tension, the baby was doing circus acrobatics deep in her womb.

The galley-style kitchen was separated from the living space by a wall, but she could hear him rattling around in the fridge. He reappeared a second later with a bottled water for her and a beer for himself, and though she'd assumed he would sit in the chair opposite her, he sat down beside her on the sofa instead.

The urge to touch him, to scoot closer and lean into him—to knock him onto his back and climb all over him—was as strong as ever. She longed for him to take her into his arms and hold her, promise her that everything would be okay. Make love to her until the last four months no longer mattered.

All he said was, "I can't let you leave again."

She should have known he wouldn't give up. He was the kind of man who was used to getting his way.

He would just have get unused to it.

"It's not your decision to make."

"The hell it isn't," he said, and his sharp tone startled her. He'd never so much as raised his voice in her presence, though at times she may have deserved it.

"Fatherhood doesn't start after the baby is born," he told her. "You robbed me of the opportunity to share the experience of your pregnancy with you."

Just when she thought she couldn't feel like a bigger jerk, he had to go and say that. And he was absolutely right. She had robbed him of all sorts of things. And robbed herself of sharing the experience with someone who actually gave a damn. Unlike her mom, who spent the first month and a half trying to convince her to "get rid of the *problem*."

Lucy had also robbed herself of the most basic creature comforts. Her mom's couch, where she had been sleeping the past four months, was miserably uncomfortable. She woke most mornings with either intense lower back pain or a severely kinked neck. Sometimes both. The idea of sleeping in a bed again, getting a peaceful night's rest, was alluring. But what would it do to her heart?

She reminded herself yet again that this was not about what she wanted. Or couldn't have. She needed to do what was best for the baby, and for now that meant taking care of herself. Tony could help her with that.

"Hypothetically, suppose I do agree to live here with you," she said. "I would have to have my own room."

"Or you could share mine." His hand came to rest on her thigh. She didn't have to see his face to know the expression he wore, and that it had the ability to melt her in seconds flat. Hadn't she promised herself that she was through making irresponsible decisions?

Tempting as it might have been, for the sake of her own pride, she couldn't go back to the way things used to be. At least in the past there had been some hope that someday things would change, that he could fall in love with her, but now she knew that would never happen. If she was going to stay here, in his apartment, they would have to establish some boundaries. Like, *no* fooling around.

She took his hand and set it on his own leg. "I think for the baby's sake we should keep our relationship platonic. So things don't get confusing."

"You can't blame a guy for trying," he said, and this time she did look at him, which was monumentally stupid. Curse him and his captivating smile. His deep-set, bedroom eyes.

"You can have my room," he told her. "I'll sleep on the fold-out in my office."

Before she could object, his cell phone started to ring. He pulled it out of his pants pocket and checked the screen, cursing under his breath. "It's *Nonno,*" he said, rising from the sofa and heading toward the kitchen. "I have to take this."

Lucy had never actually met Tony's grandfather, but she'd heard so many stories about him, in a way she felt as if she already knew him. It occurred to her that she hadn't seen him at the wedding. According to Tony, his grandfather—and before she passed away, his grandmother—had been present for every significant event in his life.

Why not his wedding?

The call barely lasted a minute before Tony hung up. "It was my mom," he said, shoving the phone back into his pocket. "She's at *Nonno*'s cleaning up. She wanted to make sure everything was okay. They want us to come by their house tomorrow to talk."

The idea of facing his parents, especially so soon, left her weak with terror. It must have shown on her face because Tony said, "Don't worry. I told her we had things to work through first, and I would let her know when it would be a good time for us to meet."

How about never? Could they meet then?

If she'd had a crystal ball, and could have seen the way events would unfold, she never would have left Chicago in the first place. She would have handled the situation like an adult instead of a lovesick adolescent. So why delay the inevitable? All she could do is apologize and hope they would take pity on her.

"I'd like to get this over with sooner rather than later," she told Tony.

"There's no rush."

"I'm responsible for this mess. I need to own up to it."

"Don't you think you're being a little hard on yourself?"

Was she? "Imagine how you would feel if your son was getting married and some woman you'd never even met showed up claiming she was pregnant with his baby. Wouldn't you want to know who she is? What she's up to?"

"You're talking like you're in this alone. I'm sure you've heard the phrase 'It takes two to tango.' I'm just as responsible."

She doubted his family would see it that way. "We shouldn't put this off."

He shrugged and said, "If that's what you want."

It wasn't about what she wanted. It was the right thing to do. "Is your grandfather okay?"

The question seemed to puzzle him. "Why do you ask?"

"I didn't see him at the service today. I thought he might not be well."

"He's fine. Just stubborn."

She wasn't sure what that had to do with it, but before she could ask, Tony's phone rang again. He pulled it out and checked the screen, muttered a curse, and rejected the call. He didn't even have time to slide the phone back into his pocket before it began to ring again. Once again he rejected the call, and this time he switched his phone to silent, muttering under his breath as he turned to Lucy. "So, are you staying?"

"I should probably tell my mom that I won't be needing a ride home from the airport, or the use of her couch," Lucy said.

Tony frowned. "She made you sleep on the *couch?*"

"It was that or the floor." Which frankly could not have been any less comfortable, though she shuddered to imagine the horrors residing in the fibers of the ancient, threadbare carpet. Her mom's friends—if you could call them that—were a motley crew of drug addicts and alcoholics.

"She couldn't take the couch and let her pregnant daughter use the bed?" Tony asked.

If he knew the kind of lifestyle her mom lead, he wouldn't blame Lucy for not wanting to get anywhere near her mattress. Lord only knew what she might catch.

But he didn't know much about her family, and she preferred to keep it that way. Tony knew that she and her mom hadn't had much, but he had no idea how rotten Lucy's childhood had been. The constant moving from one dumpy, cockroach-infested place to another. Sometimes going hungry for days because there was no money for food. The endless flow of men through her mom's revolving bedroom door.

But that was all in the past. It had happened, now it was over, and Lucy had moved on.

When she and Tony talked, it was usually about him and his work, or his family. Everything she had ever told him about her life, from birth to the present, wouldn't take more than a ten-minute conversation. He knew she didn't see her father, but he didn't know why. And all he knew of her mom was that she and Lucy had never gotten along.

He didn't know that starting when Lucy was eight, her mom would leave her alone while she went out, and often wouldn't return till morning. He didn't know how many of her mom's male "friends" had watched Lucy with a lascivious smile, said lewd and inappropriate things. Her mom used to say that it was Lucy's own fault. That she was inviting the attention by putting out "signals." And at the time, being a naive and gullible preteen, Lucy had believed her. She still wasn't sure if on some fundamental, primitive level, she was destined to be like her mom. Maybe she was hardwired that way, and it was inevitable. Only time would tell.

She wondered what Tony would think of her if he knew the truth. If he knew the kind of background she came from, and the questionable origin of the baby's genetics. What would his family think?

Tony handed her his phone, saying gently but firmly, "I won't make you sleep on the couch. Make the call."

It boiled down to what was best for the baby. So she made the call.

Three

Though he was technically on his honeymoon for the next seven days, Tony had some personal business to deal with, so the following morning he went first to the gym, then into the office. He knew full well that at some point during the course of the day he would be accosted by nearly every member of his family. After repeated calls and texts that had gone unanswered they had gotten the hint and stopped bugging him around ten o'clock p.m. last night. And started right back up this morning at eight. He loved his family. He knew that any one of them would be there for him in a pinch. They were just too damned nosy. An Italian trait, he was sure. Or maybe all big families were like that. Either way, he was tired of people being all up in his business, all the time.

He was going to have to deal with them eventually, and shy of calling a press conference, this was the easiest, not to mention quickest, way to deal with this. The alternative to work was staying home twiddling his thumbs until Lucy woke up. Yesterday, after they had a carry-out Chinese dinner, she laid down to take a short rest, and had been sound asleep ever since. Over twelve hours when he left for the gym.

He still couldn't fathom how Lucy's mom could make her pregnant daughter sleep on the couch. He knew they didn't get along well, but that was just cruel. If she didn't want to give up her own bed, couldn't she have at least sprung for an air mattress? He didn't know much about the woman. Lucy's family was an off-limits subject, but meeting her mom seemed inevitable now that he was about to be the father of her grandchild.

It still hadn't completely sunk in that in three months he was going to be somebody's parent. He and Lucy still had so much to talk about, so many decisions to make. He wasn't even sure where to begin.

Tony's secretary buzzed him. "Rob and Nick are here. They say it's urgent."

He sighed. *And so it begins.*

With a sigh of resignation, he looked at the time on his computer monitor. Nine-fifteen. That hadn't taken long. "Send them in."

Here we go—round one.

The door opened and his cousins stepped into his office. It was hard to believe that just six months ago they had all been childless bachelors. Now two of them were married and all three were expecting babies. And it was all because of *Nonno.*

"So," Nick said, making himself comfortable in the chair opposite Tony's desk. "Should I clear my calendar?"

"For what?"

"Your next wedding," Rob said, standing behind Nick, his arms folded.

As if. "Don't hold your breath."

Nick looked surprised. "You're not going to marry her? Mr. Responsibility? You always do the right thing."

"As far along as she is, I figured you would have set a date by now," Rob told him.

"I'm working on it."

"Did you find out why she left?" Nick asked. "And why it took her so long to tell you about the baby?"

"And are you sure it's yours?" Rob said.

"Yes, I'm sure that it's mine. As for why she left, and why she came back when she did, that is between her and me."

"I assume she's claiming that it was an accident," Rob said.

"It *was* an accident. Lucy wasn't any more anxious than I was to settle down."

Rob came back with, "Or so she says."

"It's the truth."

"How can you be sure?" Nick asked. "Maybe this is some elaborate setup."

Lucy didn't have a devious bone in her body. "It's not. She had every intention of going back to Florida last night. She didn't even bring a change of clothes."

"Maybe she was betting you would ask her to stay."

"Ask? I practically had to *beg* her to stay in Chicago and move in with me. She flat-out refused to marry me."

"You proposed?" Rob said.

Tony nodded. "I told her I thought it was best for the baby."

Nick's eyebrows rose. "And she said no? I can't imagine why."

"I know how it sounds, but Lucy made it very clear from the time we met that she doesn't want anything exclusive. She's incredibly independent, not to mention practical. Sentiments of love would only scare her farther away."

"Is it a boy?" Rob asked.

"We don't know yet."

"If it is?" Nick said.

"Yes, I'm taking the money. Why wouldn't I?" It was his ticket to freedom. It would benefit him, Lucy and the baby.

"How's that going to happen if she won't marry you?"

"You have to understand, it's different for us. You guys are happily married to women you love. You gave up millions of dollars to prove that to them."

"You don't love Lucy?" Nick asked.

"What I feel is irrelevant. But I do know how Lucy feels, and she happens to be the one calling all the shots right now."

"So you're just going to live together?" Rob asked.

"For now. At least until the baby is born."

"Then what?"

"She's been back less than twenty-four hours. We haven't planned that far ahead yet. We have time."

"You think so?" Nick said.

"Yes, I do."

"Terri is barely showing and she already has the kid on a waiting list for preschool."

Preschool? *"No way."*

"It's not like it was when we were kids," Rob said. "For any hope of getting a kid into a good college, you have to get them into a good private primary school first, and to do that they have to go to the right preschool."

Tony wasn't even sure if he would want to put his child in private school. As a kid, he would have given anything to go to public school, if for no other reason than to have a little privacy, and anonymity. Any childhood mishaps or embarrassments had been fodder for the entire family. Every time he tried to shirk the rules, it always got back to his parents somehow. He'd had no choice but to behave. Not that he would have been a delinquent otherwise, but being the second oldest cousin—Nick's sister

Jessica beating him out by a year and a half—he'd been held to a higher standard his entire life.

"They look up to you," his dad used to tell him, and being the oldest of the three brothers, Antonio Sr. understood sacrifice. "It's your responsibility to set a good example."

That's how it was in the Caroselli family. No sacrifice was too large. Working for Caroselli Chocolate hadn't been Tony's first choice as a career. It hadn't been his second or third, either, but he fell in line, because that was what families did. Or so he used to think. He was getting tired of playing by their rules.

He was inching closer to forty every day. When did he get to start living his life the way *he* wanted to? When he was *Nonno*'s age?

"I think Lucy and I will just have to take this one day at a time," he told his cousins. "Which would be much easier to do if everyone would just give us the time and the space we need to figure this out."

"Everyone means well," Nick said.

That didn't change the fact that they were only making things more stressful.

"There's another matter we came to talk to you about," Rob said. "We have concerns about Rose."

Rose Goldwyn, the daughter of *Nonno*'s secretary, had come to them last fall looking for a job. Because of her mother, Phyllis's, twenty-plus years of dedicated service to Caroselli Chocolate, they'd felt obligated to hire her. Unfortunately, Rose was nothing like her mother. She did her job, but unlike Phyllis, who had been like a part of the Caroselli family until she retired, Rose didn't fit in. There was something about her that just seemed a little…off. Lately Tony had come to realize that it was an opinion shared by a good majority of the family, and most of her coworkers.

"Megan pulled me aside yesterday," Rob told him. Megan, Rob's younger sister, had just bought her first home and brought Rose in as her roommate. "She said she's a little creeped out by Rose's recent behavior."

"*Recent* behavior? She's creeped me out since the day she was hired," Nick said. He was one of those guys who got along with practically everyone. If he thought something was off about Rose, they would be wise to listen.

"Meg said that Rose seems unusually interested in the family," Rob told them. "She asks a lot of questions about *Nonno* and *Nonna*."

"What kind of questions?" Tony asked.

"What they were like, did they have a good marriage?"

That *was* odd. "What does she care about our grandparents' marriage? How could that possibly be relevant to her?"

"It gets stranger. She asked if Meg had any old family movies."

"I suppose this would be a good time to mention that Terri and I caught her coming from the direction of *Nonno*'s study on the day of our wedding," Nick said. "Rose claimed she was looking for the bathroom and got lost, but then she scurried down the stairs without using the bathroom. I figured she was just nervous being at a family function for the first time. It can be a little overwhelming for an outsider. But Terri was convinced that she was lying."

Rob muttered a curse. "A couple of months ago Carrie caught Rose red-handed trying to jimmy the lock on my dad's office door."

And they were just hearing about this now? "I would

think you might have mentioned something as important as someone breaking into the CEO's office," Tony said.

"She claimed there was a paper in there that she needed, something my dad's secretary left for her. She said she forgot to grab it before my dad left and locked his office. She was afraid she would get into trouble if she didn't take care of it. Then out of the blue she got a call saying she didn't need to do it after all."

"Sounds like she always has an excuse."

"Carrie said she looked guilty."

"All the more reason to report it," Nick said.

"I didn't want to get Rose in trouble if she hadn't done anything wrong. I meant to look into it, then we found out that Carrie was pregnant, and I totally forgot to follow through."

"Understandable," Nick said.

"No kidding," Tony mumbled, and Rob chuckled.

"Do we even know for sure that Rose is Phyllis's daughter?" Nick asked. "It's not like we can ask Phyllis since she's dead. Rose could be an impostor. She could be a spy going after company secrets. She could be an undercover reporter working on an exposé."

"An exposé about chocolate?" Tony couldn't think of anything less interesting. "*Why?* Or is there something else going on here that I don't know about?"

"If there is, I don't know about it, either," Rob said. "I only know that Meg is worried. And that has me worried."

"We could take it to our parents, tell them what we know," Nick said.

"Why don't we do a little digging first?" Rob said. "I don't want to get her in trouble if her only crime is being a little odd."

"It's your call," Tony told him.

"Give me a week or two," Rob said.

Tony found himself hoping that Rob did discover some nefarious activity. With any luck it would take the focus off him for a while. At least until he figured out what to do. Lucy would marry him eventually, of that he was positive. It was just a matter of wearing her down and making her see reason.

The rich and salty scent of frying bacon woke Lucy from a deep sleep with a smile on her face. Tony almost always made her breakfast when she spent the night. Even if he only had time to toast bread or pour her a bowl of cereal before he left for work. He kept her favorite kind around for such occasions, which had been more frequent in the weeks before she left.

Until just now, Lucy had never stopped to consider what a nice gesture that was. In fact, he did an awful lot of nice things for her. She couldn't help feeling that she'd taken him for granted.

She wouldn't be making that mistake again.

She pried her lids open and looked at the clock. She blinked several times, sure that her eyes were playing tricks on her. It couldn't possibly be 11:30 a.m. That would mean that she'd slept for almost *eighteen* hours.

On the bedside table her phone chirped, alerting her that she had new text message. She reached over and grabbed it.

Ugh.

There were half a dozen text messages. All from her mom.

Lucy had taken the coward's way out last night. Instead of calling, she'd messaged her mom to say that she wouldn't need a lift from the airport after all, and she'd be staying in Chicago a little longer than expected.

How long and with who? had been her mom's immediate response.

As tempting as it was to throw her mom's words back at her—*wouldn't marry a woman like me, my ass*—that sort of thing always seemed to blow up in her face. After careful consideration, Lucy decided that it wouldn't be worth the temporary feeling of satisfaction. The less her mom knew at this point, the better.

She texted back, A friend, not sure how long, no time to discuss it. If Lucy believed for a second her mom was concerned for her well-being, she would have answered. She knew better.

She rolled out of bed and looked around for her clothes, then remembered that Tony had offered to wash them for her. He must have forgotten to take them out of the dryer.

She grabbed his flannel robe from the back of the closet door where he'd always kept it. The scent of his soap and aftershave tickled her nose as she pulled it on over the white undershirt he'd given her to wear last night. While the shirt was so huge it hung to just above her knees, the robe didn't quite make it all the way around her tummy.

With the baby doing aerobics on her bladder, her first stop was the bathroom. Tony used to keep a hot pink toothbrush for her in the vanity drawer, but he wouldn't have kept it all this time. Would he?

She slid the drawer open, gasping softly when she saw it lying there next to a brand-new tube of her favorite toothpaste. How did he remember that? And why keep her toothbrush if he was planning to marry someone else?

One thing at a time, she reminded herself. She brushed her teeth and finger-combed her hair into place. She had always worn her hair on the short side, but her current style, a messy-ish pixie cut, was by far the easiest to maintain, and she knew Tony liked it that way. Her mom claimed it made Lucy look like an elf. The way Lucy looked at it, the less she had to fuss over herself, the more time she would have to fuss over the baby.

Knowing they had much to discuss, Lucy was ravaged by nerves as she walked to the kitchen. To Tony. But as she rounded the corner and saw who it was standing at the stove, she wished she would have stayed in bed. She froze in the kitchen doorway, wondering if she could sneak back to the bedroom, but Tony's mom must have had eyes in the back of her head.

"Sleep well?" she asked Lucy, still facing away, using a fork to lift several crispy slices of bacon from the pan onto a paper towel. On the counter beside the stove sat a plate with golden French toast made from thick, crusty, Italian bread. Just like the kind Tony used to make her.

Her mouth started to water and her stomach howled for nourishment.

"Where is Tony?" Lucy asked her. *And what the heck are you doing here making me breakfast?*

"He was gone when I got here," she said, patting away the extra grease from the bacon with an edge of the paper towel. In slip-on flats, she was just about the same height as Lucy, but that was where any similarity ended.

"When was that?" Lucy asked.

"Thirty minutes ago, give or take." She put the bacon on the plate and turned to Lucy, giving her a quick once-over, one brow slightly raised. "I hope you're hungry."

She held the plate out and Lucy took it, so nervous her hands were trembling. If his mom noticed, she was kind enough not to point it out. She gestured to the table and said, "Sit down. Eat it while it's hot."

Obediently Lucy sat. It was like her worst nightmare come true. Coming face-to-face with the mother of the man whose baby she was carrying, and doing it not only alone, but in *his* T-shirt and robe. Could this get any worse?

"Maybe I should call Tony," Lucy said, tugging the robe tighter around her belly.

"Why don't you and I chat for a while?" his mom said, taking a seat across from Lucy. "I'd like to know a little bit about my future daughter-in-law."

Oh, boy, this was going to fun to explain. "Maybe we should wait for Tony."

She dismissed the idea with a flutter of perfectly man-icured nails, her smile patient yet firm. "Tell me about yourself. How did you meet my son?"

"We met at the bar where I was working," she said, leaving it at that.

When Tony's mom realized that was all Lucy planned to tell her, she asked, "How long have you been seeing each other?"

"Mrs. Caroselli—"

"It's Sarah. Or Mom. Whichever you're more com-fortable with."

Mom? She was sure she wasn't ready for that. "I don't want you to get the wrong idea. Tony and I, we're not... we were never anything but friends. I know this will be hard to believe, but I didn't come here intending to break up the wedding. I didn't even know it was a wedding. I had heard that he was getting married and knew I should tell him about the baby. I was planning to go right back to Florida after I talked to him."

Looking amused, Sarah said, "And how did Tony feel about that?"

She shifted in her seat. She didn't want to offend Sarah, or come off as a bitch. Or even worse, seem as if she was hiding something. But it didn't seem right talking about this without Tony present. "Suffice it to say that we have a lot to work out."

"In other words, mind my own business," Sarah said, looking more amused than angry.

"Sarah, I can only imagine what you must think of me. What your *entire* family must think."

"Lucy...can I call you Lucy?"

"O-of course. Absolutely."

"Take my word for it, *anyone* who saw the look on your face when you stepped into the room yesterday knew you were just as stunned to see us as we were to see you. I would say, considering my son's reaction when he saw you, and his demand that you announce your business to everyone, you two must have a very complicated relationship."

She had *no* idea.

"You don't have to answer that," she said. "Not only is it not my business, all that really matters to me is that you stopped my son from marrying that horrible woman."

Four

Horrible woman? Lucy blinked in surprise. "You didn't like Alice?"

"No one did. To be honest, I don't even know if Tony liked her all that much. Or she him."

What? "Why would they get married if they didn't like each other?"

"That's what everyone has been trying to figure out. We all assumed that she was pregnant."

Lucy's breath caught in her throat, and her stomach did a violent flip-flop. It had never occurred to her that Alice could be pregnant, too. It would explain the rushed marriage. But what were the odds that he would knock up two different women accidentally within months of each other? And would Tony let Alice go back to New York knowing she was carrying his child?

"Could she be?" Lucy asked, terrified that Sarah might actually say yes.

"When I saw the way she was slamming back champagne yesterday before the service, I came right out and asked her. She is not."

Thank God.

"I was relieved as well. She never struck me as the maternal type," Sarah said. "Children seemed to make her uncomfortable."

"Not everyone is cut out to be a parent," Lucy told her. "Some people are too selfish."

"Some are indeed," Sarah agreed. "But not you. I can tell."

Lucy laid a hand on her tummy and a content smile tugged at the corners of her mouth. "This baby means everything to me."

"Do you know if it's a boy or girl?"

She shook her head. "It feels like a boy, though."

"When I was pregnant with Tony, I knew he was a boy. Will you find out the sex of the baby beforehand?"

"At first I wanted to know, but I've been thinking about it and I kind of want to be surprised. I've waited this long. What's another three months?"

"I like surprises," Sarah said. "Most of the time."

Lucy wondered if this was one of those times. "I'm a little confused about something."

"What?"

"You have every reason not to like me, or at the very least to be suspicious of me."

"You're absolutely right. I do."

"Then why are you being so nice to me?"

The question seemed to amuse Sarah. "Did Tony ever tell you that I was three months pregnant with him when I married my husband?"

Lucy shook her head. That would certainly explain Sarah's willingness to accept her.

"My in-laws came to Chicago straight off the boat and had very strict, traditional moral beliefs," Sarah said. "Suffice it to say that when I turned up pregnant, they were not happy with me. In fact, they were so furious they not only refused to pay for a penny of the wedding, but my husband had to beg them to attend."

"Did they?"

"Yes, but in retrospect, I almost wished they hadn't. They made no secret of how they felt about me in front of my entire family and all of my friends. It was awkward. Not to mention heartbreaking. That first year, what should have been the happiest time in my life, was miserable and lonely."

That was so sad. "But things got better?"

"It took several years before I felt truly comfortable with them, like a part of the family. Eventually Angelica and I even became friends. It turns out we had a lot in common. We both love to cook. We were both born in Italy, although my family originated from the north."

Which explained the blond hair and fair complexion. And meant that Tony was one hundred percent pure-blooded Italian. "It's too bad it had to be that way."

"To this day I still find it terribly sad that we wasted so many years at odds. Being accepted by her from the start would have meant the world to me. I always swore that if I ever found myself in a similar situation with one of my children, I would give the person in question the benefit of the doubt, get to know him or her before I pass judgment. That's what I'm doing."

"Thank you." Lucy had never been much of a crier—what if she started, then wasn't able to stop?—but tears burned her eyes. It was good to know that she had an ally. Even if Sarah was only one ally among many enemies. Maybe if she accepted Lucy, the rest of the family would fall in line. Or at least be a little less judgmental.

"Now that we have that settled…" Sarah nudged Lucy's plate closer. "Eat your breakfast! You're skinny as a rail."

"I know I'm too thin," Lucy said, her cheeks burning with shame. She'd been trying to eat healthy, for the baby. Unfortunately food—especially the healthy kind—had been in short supply at her mom's place, and with Lucy having no job, so was money. She did the best she could on what little she had.

"Don't worry, I intend to fatten you up," Sarah said. "As only a true Italian mama can."

It would be nice to have someone take care of her for a change. And she wished she and Sarah could be friends, but that would mean telling her things about herself, things no one in Tony's family could ever know. Not if there was any hope of them truly accepting her. Even worse, they might not accept the baby. She couldn't let that happen. She wanted her child to have a big, loving, supportive family. Just like Lucy had always wanted. Prayed for even, for all the good it had done.

It may not have been an option for her anymore, but her baby would have it. She would see to that.

At any cost.

Around two that afternoon, of what was turning into the longest day in Tony's life, he was in his car and heading home when he was summoned by *Nonno*. Everyone in the family knew that when *Nonno* requested an audience, it was wise to cooperate. Which is how Tony found himself sitting in his grandfather's study, waiting for what he assumed would be a firm lecture. Though about what, he wasn't sure. It could be any number of things.

Nonno sat in his wingback leather chair beside the picture window overlooking the park across the street, his gnarled, bony hands folded in his lap. To the casual observer, *Nonno* looked harmless. A gentle old man with a twinkle in his eye. Tony knew better. Despite his frail physical condition he was still sharp as a tack, and ran the family with an iron fist. Tony's dad and his brothers liked to believe that they were the ones in control, but it was only an illusion. *Nonno* was always there pulling the strings. At times Tony wondered how his father had managed not to lose his sanity for all these years of being under the old man's thumb. To live someone else's dream and never make his own mark. How could he stand it?

"So, this girl who broke up your wedding," *Nonno* said, getting right to the point. "It's your baby she's carrying?"

"Yes."

"You're positive?"

"I trust Lucy. She's a good friend."

Nonno winked. "More than that, it would seem."

"I know it might seem that way...."

"Is the child a boy?"

"We don't know for sure yet, but Lucy seems to think so."

Nonno nodded thoughtfully. "If she's right, you could be a very wealthy man."

If only. "There's just one little problem."

"Or not so little, I'm thinking, by your troubled expression."

"Lucy refuses to marry me."

The news seemed to amuse him. "Did she tell you why she wouldn't marry you?"

"She doesn't want the family to think that she got pregnant on purpose to trap me."

"Did she?"

The question threw him. "No. *Hell no.* She's not like that."

"We'll just make sure everyone else in the family knows the truth, and that should solve the problem. Yes?"

"I don't think so."

"This woman, she loves you?"

Technically, *Nonno* had never said Tony had to be in love with the mother of the child, or she him, to inherit the money. He only said they had to be married. "Lucy and I don't really have that kind of relationship. We're friends."

Nonno's brows rose again. "Are you suggesting that it was an immaculate conception?"

"Of course not. We were just…" Just what? Fooling around?

Oh, good God, was he actually discussing his sex life with his ninety-two-year-old grandfather? Just when he thought he couldn't sink any lower, if he wasn't careful, they were going to revoke his Man Card. "Are you familiar with the term *friends with benefits?*"

"I'm not *that* old," *Nonno* said, looking amused. "But in my day we called it something different."

"Well, that's me and Lucy. Friends with benefits."

"So she's good enough to sleep with, and to carry your child, but not to marry?"

Had *Nonno* not heard a thing he'd said? "I *want* to marry her. I've *asked* her to marry me. I can't force her."

"You told her you love her?"

What part of *friends with benefits* did he not understand? "I told her that I thought it was what's best for the baby."

"And still she said no?"

"I don't know what else to do," Tony said. Maybe *Nonno* would be willing to compromise if Tony promised him the baby would have the Caroselli name. "You know, even if I didn't marry her, the baby would take my last name. He would still be a Caroselli."

Though it took effort, *Nonno* leaned forward in his

chair, head cocked a notch to the left. "Are you asking me to amend our agreement?"

"You would still get the heir you were hoping for."

"That is true…." He trailed off, looking thoughtful, and Tony had real hope that he would agree, but then he shook his head and said, "No, I can't do that."

He *could* do it, but he wouldn't.

"It wouldn't be right. If you want the trust, you'll marry her." *Nonno*'s tone said the matter was closed.

"How? She dug in her heels and she won't budge."

"You'll think of something. I have faith in you."

That faith may have been misplaced. Lucy was almost as bullheaded as *Nonno*.

"Bring her to me," *Nonno* said. "I'll talk to her."

Tony couldn't imagine a worse idea. "I don't think—"

"I do," *Nonno* said firmly, any further discussion unnecessary. He liked things done a certain way. His way. "Bring her to me tomorrow, here in my study. At three p.m."

This had the potential to be a really bad idea. "I'll bring her. Just…promise me you'll go easy on her. I know you have a strict set of moral standards, but just remember what year it is. Don't do to her what you did to my mom."

Nonno's brows rose. "You know about that?"

"Of course I do. I may have been little, but I wasn't stupid. I knew that you and *Nonna* didn't approve of her. I didn't understand why. Which I think is both good and bad. I still don't know why you were so harsh on her. What did she do that was so terrible?"

Nonno looked away, out the window. "There are some things that we don't discuss. For the good of the family."

For the good of the family, or his own selfish reasons?

Either way, Lucy had done nothing to warrant his wrath. "Lucy is confused and scared and I don't want to make her feel any worse than she already does. I will not abide by anyone trying to intimidate her. That includes you."

Tony had never dared raise his voice when speaking to his grandfather, or issued an outright order. And though he braced for the fallout, *Nonno* looked more intrigued than angry.

"Is that so?" he said, almost as if he were taunting Tony, daring him to defy the head of the family. Tony refused to be intimidated. He never understood why his dad allowed his parents to treat their daughter-in-law so poorly, but Tony wouldn't abide by it. It was his duty, as the father of Lucy's child, to protect her, not throw her under the bus. She'd been through enough.

"The last thing I want is to disrespect you, but Lucy is my responsibility now."

"Even when she refuses to marry you?"

"No matter what."

Nonno actually smiled. "In that case, I promise that I will treat her with respect and kindness."

Wow, that was almost *too* easy. What was the catch? "We'll come by at three tomorrow."

"I'll speak to Lucy alone," *Nonno* said.

And there it was. "*Nonno*—"

"Drop her off, and come back an hour later to fetch her. Now leave me. I need to rest."

Tony didn't like the idea of leaving Lucy alone with *Nonno,* but once he dismissed a guest, the conversation was over. He just had to trust that his grandfather would honor his promise and treat Lucy well. After so many years of loyal service to the company, at the expense of his own aspirations, not only did Tony deserve it. He had earned it.

* * *

As he parallel parked in a spot on the street about a block from his building, Tony swore that his next apartment would have tenant parking. Some conveniences were worth the extra expense. Especially on those snowy Chicago nights when he came home late from the office. With the baby coming they would need more space anyway. Maybe he should think about apartment hunting sooner rather than later.

As he crossed the street, Tony noticed a familiar white Mercedes parked down the block.

Oh, no. She wouldn't have.

Picking up speed, he jogged the rest of the way, and rather than wait for the elevator, took the stairwell up to his floor. He didn't see her immediately when he stepped inside, but he knew that perfume anywhere.

Exasperated, he shouted, "Mother!"

She stepped out of the kitchen drying her hands on a dish towel, looking casually sophisticated in beige wool slacks and a rose cable-knit sweater, with her mostly white hair pulled back from a face still youthful even though she'd just celebrated her sixty-third birthday. "Hello, dear."

Hello, dear, my foot.

"Really, Mom?" He shrugged out of his jacket and tossed it over the back of the couch. "You couldn't have waited a couple days like I asked?"

With a sigh, she picked his jacket up and hung it in the closet, telling him, "And you couldn't have stayed home from the office for a day? When your father called to tell me that you had come into work, all I could think was that you left that poor girl all alone. With no transportation and, as I guessed, no food."

She made it sound as if Lucy would have starved to death had she not intervened. "Where is she?"

"Taking a shower. I made her a healthy breakfast."

Breakfast? He looked at his watch. "Mom, it's almost four in the afternoon. How long have you been here?"

"What difference does that make? You can't just abandon a pregnant woman in an apartment with nothing but sour milk, shriveled carrots, moldy cheese and Dijon mustard. She needs a balanced diet. It's a good thing your father called me, and a good thing I still have your spare key."

He put a clamp down on his anger. "Did you at least try knocking first?"

"Of course. No one answered."

So she just let herself in. In her world, that probably made perfect sense. She had an issue with boundaries. The issue being that she had none. "That typically means that either no one is home, or whoever is home would rather not be disturbed."

"Well, lucky for both of us she was still asleep. She didn't have to wake up to an empty home with an equally empty refrigerator. You're welcome."

She meant well, he knew she did, but she still drove him nuts. Although in retrospect, she had a valid point. He should have made sure Lucy had everything she needed before he left. He wasn't used to being responsible for anyone but himself.

He relented and told his mom, "I appreciate you coming by, but I've got it from here."

"This was a novelty for me," she said. "It's not often I get to meet your girlfriends."

"She's not—" He shook his head. "Never mind."

"Tony, sweetheart." She laid a hand on his chest and patted affectionately, regarding him as if he were still a clueless kid. "Promise me you'll be patient with her. It's a very confusing time. She's going to need all the support she can get."

A couple of hours with Lucy and she thought she knew her? He'd known Lucy for over a year, and he still had no idea what went on in her head. She was one of the most self-sufficient women he knew, and one of the most insecure. "I appreciate the advice. And I know you mean well, but you don't even know her."

"Oh, sweetheart," his mom said, her smile sad. "I *was* her. I know exactly what she's going through."

Come to think of it, she probably did. And it would be in his best interest to listen to her. "So what do I do?"

"Be there for her. Protect her. And just give her time. She needs you, even if she's afraid to show it. And for heaven's sake, take her shopping. She showed up empty-handed. There must be a million things she needs."

"Like…?"

"Shampoo, deodorant…a hairbrush. And some decent-fitting clothes."

These were things he should have realized himself. What the hell was wrong with him? Had seeing her again and learning about the baby really zapped him so hard? He was acting like a selfish ass. This was why he avoided serious relationships. He was no good at it. Perhaps because the longest relationship of any kind that he'd had with a woman was with Lucy. It was so…easy. She had her life and he had his and every so often those two worlds would collide. It was a pretty cool arrangement. One that he'd thought was working for the both of them.

His mom to the rescue again.

He lifted her hand off his chest and kissed the back of it. "I will, Mom. I promise. And thank you."

She smiled and patted his cheek, making him feel six years old. "My good boy."

That was him, always the obedient son. But maybe it wasn't so bad this time. She may have driven him nuts from time to time, but her intentions were good. She did it out of love. It was easy to forget that.

"I'm going to go talk to Lucy."

"And I'm going to go home. Your father promised to take me out to dinner tonight. Call if you need anything."

"I will."

After she left he walked to his bedroom, hoping his mother's visit hadn't been too traumatic for Lucy. And he was so used to having her around, he didn't stop to think about her privacy as he opened the door.

Five

Though she wasn't typically shy about her body, and Tony had seen her naked more times than she could count, when Lucy turned to see him standing in the bedroom doorway, her hands flew up to cover herself. Her bra and panties covered the essentials, yet for some reason she felt utterly exposed. Then she realized that no one other than the clinic doctor had seen her undressed in the past four months.

What if Tony found her body revolting?

Maybe under the circumstances that wouldn't be such a bad thing.

"I'm sorry, I should have knocked. I didn't think…" He trailed off as his eyes settled on her stomach then went wide. "Wow, you're big."

Maybe it was the look she gave him, or his brain was just catching up to his mouth, but he quickly added, "I mean your stomach, not the rest of you. In fact, my mom is right. You are too thin." He hesitated, then added, "Although not in an unattractive way."

"Quit while you're ahead, Caroselli," she told him, before he dug himself in any deeper. For a man so educated and sophisticated, he had this way of putting his foot in his mouth. And though he sometimes said things that made her want to smack him upside the head, she considered his cluelessness one of his most endearing qualities.

He shot her a grin that made her knees go weak and said, "I think you know what I mean."

"I do." It would have felt so natural to slide her arms around his neck, push him down on his bed. Like she had so many times before...

No, she definitely couldn't do that.

"Did he just move?"

That was an understatement. "He's been doing gymnastics all day. I think he liked that breakfast your mom made."

"It looks like it would hurt." Tony said, transfixed by her tummy. It was academic in a way. Like Pregnancy 101.

"Not usually, although sometimes he'll get a foot up under my rib cage and kick hard. That can be a little uncomfortable. And he likes to lay on my bladder."

"Can I feel?" he asked.

His bare hands on her bare stomach. Why did that sound like a really bad idea? But what was she supposed to do? Tell him no? Hadn't he missed enough already? And all because of her. From this point on she wanted him to be totally involved. She *owed* him that much. "Of course you can."

Wearing a look of childlike anticipation, he sat on the edge of the bed, bringing himself down to her level. She poked at her stomach, looking for a discernible body part for him to feel.

Tony winced. "It doesn't hurt pushing on your stomach like that?"

"Sometimes you have to give him a poke to get him

to move. I think he's on his back. Let me try…oh wait…I found him." She took Tony's hand and pressed it against her belly. "Push right here."

He applied the slightest bit of pressure where his hand lay, cringing as if he was expecting her to howl in pain.

"You won't feel anything that way. You have to really get in there and dig around."

He looked at her like she was nuts.

"I'm not kidding." She folded her hand over his and really pushed hard, until they met with something solid about an inch or so in. "Feel that?"

His eyes shot to hers. "Is that him?"

She smiled and said, "A leg I think. Sometimes it's hard to tell."

"Fascinating," he said, cupping her belly in both hands, sliding his thumbs back and forth….

He obviously wasn't doing it to excite her, but try telling that to her body. It didn't seem to know the difference. She was already on hormone overload. If she could at least put some clothes on—

Tony leaned closer, pressing his cheek against her belly, and Lucy sucked in a breath. He must have touched her there a million times, but today, as his afternoon stubble tickled her skin, she felt it like an electric shock. One that fired up her libido and sent her hormone production into overdrive.

He peered up at her through a veil of thick black lashes, wearing a look so ridiculously adorable, she melted.

"Too much?" he asked.

Yes. And no. And again please. And while you're down there…

All she said was, "Stubble."

"Sorry. Missed my afternoon shave," he said. His beard grew so aggressively, he kept an electric razor at work for touch-ups. It was those Italian genes of his. She was sure that if she looked closely enough, she could probably watch it grow.

"I hope my mom didn't give you a hard time," he said, his cheek still pressed to her belly. The tickle of his beard, the warm fan of his breath, the desire to tunnel her fingers through his hair, were almost too much to take. "She's been known to overstep her boundaries from time to time."

"The truth is, she was really nice to me. Probably more than I deserved under the circumstances."

"You did what you thought was right. No one can fault you for that."

No, she had done what was *easy.* She ran. Sticking around meant facing her mistakes, and living with the consequences. *That* was the hard part.

"I talked to my sister Chris today. I got the names and numbers of her OBGYN and pediatrician. I took the liberty and made us an appointment for tomorrow morning at nine with the former."

"I'm surprised you got us in so fast. They must have had a cancellation."

"Not necessarily." He grinned and said, "I can be very persuasive."

Tell me about it.

"After the appointment we'll go shopping. We'll get you whatever you need. And don't bother saying that you'll pay me back. This one is on me."

That was exactly what she had been about to say. And normally she would have put up at least a little bit of a fight, but she was just too darned tired. It would feel good, for once in her life, to let someone take care of her. It went against everything she had learned, but she was determined to try.

"I had an interesting visit with *Nonno* today," Tony said.

"You saw your grandfather?"

Tony nodded, the scrape of his beard creating a whole new round of sensations she shouldn't be feeling. "He called and asked me to come by."

According to Tony, when *Nonno* called, you didn't tell him no. "Is he angry with you?"

"He wants to meet you."

Her stomach bottomed out.

Her look must have said it all. "Don't worry. I made him promise to be civilized."

The fact that he'd felt it necessary to make *Nonno* promise was a bad sign. Besides, there were degrees of civilized.

"I'm sorry I left this morning," Tony said. "I should have stuck around until you woke up. And fed you. I don't know what I was thinking."

"You were thinking what you always think when I spend the night. That in the morning you go to work, and I go home. That's the way it's always been. So don't beat yourself up over it. Okay?"

"You can't deny that things are a little different now."

"They don't have to be. Why can't we just pick up where we left off?"

He peered up at her wearing that look and she knew exactly what he was thinking.

"Except for *that*."

"Damn," he said, with a grin that melted her like butter. "Can't blame a guy for trying."

No, not once or twice. But if he kept trying, she might forget to tell him no, and then where would they be? She was already pregnant, so what was the worst that could happen? She would fall *more* in love with him? Compromise her dignity a little? Shred her heart?

Piece of cake.

"The only other real difference is that I won't go home in the morning," she said.

"So what you're saying is, we'll be like roommates."

"Yes, exactly."

It was a little sad that after a year, and a pregnancy, all they had managed to progress to was roommates. Which was actually a step back from their friends with benefits status. Why did she suddenly feel as if they were going in the wrong direction?

Unfortunately, for the sake of everyone involved, including the baby, that was the only place they *could* go.

Lucy sat on the exam table, clutching together at the front a way-too-large white paper gown, waiting for Dr. Hannan. Tony sat in one of the two chairs, his long legs stretched out in front of him, checking his email on his phone. Unlike the free clinic or health department where she received her care in Florida, this place was state-of-the-art. According to Tony's sister, all of their mothers and female cousins went there.

Since leaving her alone yesterday morning, Tony had been going out of his way to be more attentive. He woke her with breakfast in bed, then, while she was in the shower, he ran a steamer over her clothes to freshen them up. It was sprinkling when they left, and though she didn't mind getting a little wet, he insisted she stay by the door while he went and got the car, which was parked a block away. At the doctor's office he dropped her by the door, where she waited while he parked, and all she could think was that this all seemed a little too good to be true. She wasn't used to being pampered this way, or any way for that matter, so she couldn't help but wait for the other shoe to drop.

"I'm curious," Lucy said, and Tony looked up from his phone.

"Like this is news to me?" he said with a grin.

"Do you miss her?"

He looked at her blankly. "Miss who?"

Really? He couldn't figure that out? "Your fiancée. *Alice*."

"Oh, her," he said, as if he'd forgotten all about her. Out of sight out of mind? Had he forgotten Lucy that quickly?

"It's been two days since you two split up and you haven't said a word about her."

"Nothing much to say."

"Is it true that you didn't like her much?"

A frown tugged down the corners of his mouth. "Let me take a wild guess. My mom told you that."

"She didn't seem to like Alice much."

"Don't look so happy about that."

Who, her? "I'm not. I swear."

His look said he thought she was full of it.

"Okay, maybe I am a little." Especially since Sarah did seem to like Lucy. For now anyway. "It's just a little…confusing."

"What is?"

"Why you would marry someone you don't love. I mean…in our case it's different. There's a baby involved."

"It's a long story," he said, eyes on his phone. One he clearly didn't want to tell her. It might have been awkward if the doctor hadn't chosen that second to open the door.

He was an older gentleman with thick silver hair and a kind face. He introduced himself and shook their hands, addressing Lucy as Mrs. Caroselli.

In her dreams maybe.

"It's Ms. Bates," she told him. "But you can call me Lucy."

"All right, Lucy," he said, skimming through her chart, which, unlike the clinic in Florida, he accessed on a laptop computer. Which reminded her that she had left her laptop in Florida. There was no point in asking her mom to send it. She'd probably already pawned it. It was outdated and on its last leg anyway. Maybe Tony would let her use his computer from time to time. If only to access her online journal. She tried to write it in every day.

"Lie down, feet in the stirrups," the doctor said. "Let's do an exam, and then we can talk in my office."

He examined her, poking and prodding, firing off questions. Many of them the same questions the nurse had asked as if maybe they were trying to trip her up and catch her in a lie.

Any nausea? Not really. High blood pressure? Never. Prenatal vitamins? Just the over-the-counter kind. Does the baby move around a lot? Like an Olympic gymnast.

Dr. Hannan was incredibly thorough.

Tony stood by the head of the table, absently rubbing her shoulder, looking fascinated and a maybe little horrified as the doctor did the internal exam, then measured her tummy and listened to the baby's heartbeat.

Then he was done.

He made a few notes on her chart and said, "Get dressed and meet me in my office down the hall, last door on the left."

"That was interesting," Tony said, when he was gone, turning away so Lucy could get dressed in private. "I didn't think it would be so…invasive. You have to do that every month?"

She tugged on her jeans. "Probably not until I'm closer to my due date. Typically it's just a tummy check."

When she was dressed they walked down the hall to Dr. Hannan's office. He offered them a seat, then Lucy waited for the usual report. She was fine, the baby was fine. Yada yada. But the doctor was wearing a frown that said maybe everything wasn't fine this time.

"I don't like what I'm seeing here," he said.

Lucy sucked in a quiet breath and Tony went tense beside her.

"What do you mean?" he asked.

"The baby isn't growing like he should be."

How could that be possible? "But…everything was fine at my last appointment," Lucy told him. "They did mention that he was on the small side, but the doctor said that's probably because *I'm* so small."

"It's more than him just being small in size. He's underdeveloped for his gestational age. I think you're both suffering from malnutrition. It could result in complications."

"Malnutrition?" Tony said, like that was the most ridiculous thing he'd ever heard. "How is that possible?"

"It's something I might see in a woman with severe morning sickness. Which you said you didn't have."

Lucy shook her head, wishing she could disappear. Or that Tony wasn't in the room. There were certain things the doctor needed to know. The same things she *didn't* want Tony to know. She could fudge it just this once, but one lie had a way of turning into two, and so on, and so on. And before she knew it, the doctor might miss some critical detail, and the baby might be born with a third eye or fifth appendage, or something even worse.

If she and Tony were going to make this shared-parenting thing work, she was going to have to be honest with him. A lie by omission was still a lie. But there were some things she just couldn't tell him. Ever. For his own good. And for hers and the baby's.

"In my experience, Caroselli babies are above average in size," Dr. Hannan said. "We could be looking at a metabolic disorder."

"What kind of disorder?" Tony asked.

"One thing at a time," the doctor told him, then asked Lucy, "How has your diet been?"

"Well…up until Sunday, not so great." She cringed at the look he gave her. As if he were thinking, *You poor stupid girl, too much of a low-life hick to know about proper nutrition.*

"I'm sure that your doctor in Florida told you the importance of a balanced diet. Now is not the time to be cutting calories."

"It's more of an availability issue," she said, and at the doctor's look of confusion added, "When I eat I make sure it's something healthy. It's just that for a couple of months money was tight."

She braced herself, expecting Tony to jump all over that one, but he didn't make a sound. Which was probably worse. She had no idea what was going on in his head.

"Give me an example of your daily intake," the doctor said. "How often did you eat?"

Oh, boy, here we go. Tony was not going to like this. "Well, I did try to eat at least once a day. Sometimes that wasn't possible. But I always bought healthy things, even if that meant quality over quantity. But from now on that won't be a problem."

"No, it won't," Tony agreed tersely. She could see that he was angry, and could she blame him? She'd put his baby's life in danger. She was angry with herself.

"I'd like you back here tomorrow for an ultrasound," Dr. Hannan told them. "If the baby looks good, I won't need to see you back for a month. But I would like you to see a nutritionist."

One more thing Tony would have to pay for. In her

lifetime she would probably never make enough money to pay him back for everything he would be doing for her.

They both shook the doctor's hand and thanked him, but Tony was silent as they checked out and made the ultrasound appointment. He didn't speak as they walked through the waiting room, or as they crossed the lobby to the door. He wasn't the type to embarrass her or himself by making a scene in front of other people, but she could feel him working up to something. He would wait until they were alone, in the privacy of the car, before he let her have it.

"Fancy meeting you two here," a familiar voice said, and they both turned to see Nick and a woman Lucy assumed to be his wife walking toward them from the rear of the lot, their hands linked. Lucy could swear she heard Tony curse under his breath.

"Hi again, Lucy," Nick said. "This my wife, Terri."

Terri smiled, which was a promising sign, and pumped Lucy's hand. She was pretty in a tomboyish way. Tall and slender with mile-long legs and an honest face. And one hell of a firm grip. "It's good to meet you, Lucy. And I mean that sincerely. Your timing Sunday was perfect. Although I'm sure that if you hadn't intervened someone else would have."

Intervened? She made it sound as if it had been Lucy's intention to break up the wedding. Did the whole family believe that? "It wasn't like that. I didn't even know about the wedding. It was kind of a fluke."

Tony shifted beside her and she could feel him getting annoyed. "Here for a checkup?" he asked Terri.

"Ultrasound," Terri said.

"We're having one tomorrow," Lucy told her.

"Do you want to know the sex of the baby?"

"No, I would rather be surprised."

"Not me. I want to be prepared when the baby is born. No green and yellow, gender neutral stuff for this kid."

"Will you find out today?"

"It's a little early, but if we're lucky we might be able to tell."

"Terri thinks it's a girl," Nick said. "But I know it's a boy."

"Well, good luck," Tony said, linking his arm with Lucy's and all but dragging her in the direction of the car.

"Nice to meet you, Lucy," Terri called after them, and Lucy waved back. Tony was walking so fast, and had such a longer stride than her, she could scarcely keep up. Thank goodness the car wasn't far away.

He opened her door for her, then walked around the back and got in. But he didn't start the engine. He just sat there, both hands gripping the wheel, his body tense.

She had a very bad feeling about this.

"It's more of an *availability* issue?" he finally said, turning to her, and she thought, *Aw, hell, here we go.*

"I should have said something—"

"Not only did your mom make you sleep on the couch," he said, interrupting her. "But she didn't feed you?"

Lucy blinked. Her *mom?* What did she have to do with this?

"My mom eats out most of the time," she told him, if eating out meant peanuts with her beer and cigarette, because that and an occasional tavern burger made up the majority of her diet. "She doesn't keep much food around. And I was pretty low on money, so…"

"You should have called me," he said. He didn't look angry exactly. It was more like…barely contained rage. Like if he didn't let off some steam soon his head might explode. "I would have taken care of you."

"I know you would have. I was wrong not to call. All I can say is I'm sorry. And I understand why you're mad at me."

He turned, looking at her like she'd just sprouted a second eye. "You think I'm mad at you?"

Duh. "How could you not be? I've messed everything up."

"Lucy, the only person I'm mad at is me."

Six

Tony felt sick to his stomach. Sick to the depths of his soul. While he was home in Chicago, wining and dining Alice—a woman he admittedly didn't even like—Lucy had been across the country literally starving, too poor to afford a basic balanced diet.

Why hadn't he gone after her? Deep down he knew that something had to be wrong, that she wouldn't just take off without a word. Because of his own stupidity and his foolish male pride, their child might be in danger.

If something were to happen to the baby, something bad, Tony would never forgive himself.

"Why would you be mad at yourself?" she asked him. "You didn't do anything wrong."

He gripped the wheel hard. "I should have been taking care of you."

"But…how could you? I left. How could you even know that I needed to be taken care of?"

He knew. He may not have wanted to admit it to himself, but he definitely knew something was wrong. "I should have been there for you."

Lucy was quiet for several seconds, then said, "I think we're doing this wrong."

"Doing what wrong?"

"This." She gestured between the two of them. "Aren't we supposed to be blaming *each other?* Yet here we both are falling all over ourselves, trying to take the blame. It's…weird."

She had a point. For him, the blame game had been responsible for the demise of more than a few budding relationships. But his relationship with Lucy was unlike any he'd ever had. "It's just who we are, I guess."

"I guess." Despite what she believed, he'd failed her. He'd let her down. It wasn't going to happen again. As far as he was concerned, for the rest of her life, Lucy would never want for a single thing. Even if she refused to marry him, he would always take care of her as the mother of his child,. And as much as he wanted to pull her into his arms and hold her, it might only push her farther away. Though it was tough, he stayed on his side of the car.

"Do you have a preference as to where you'd like to shop for clothes?" he asked, starting the car.

"I usually go to the thrift shop on Montrose," she said. "They have good stuff at that one. I find a lot of things that are new with the tags still on for super cheap."

Over his dead body.

He took her to the mall instead, to the department store where his sister and mom liked to shop. Only then did he appreciate just how frugal and disciplined she could be. She went straight to the clearance section. When she did find something she liked she would immediately come up with some reason why he shouldn't buy it for her. Why she could live comfortably without it. So different from Alice, who always seemed to have her hand out. Lucy had class, and dignity, and too much pride for her own good.

What had Elana called Alice? A bloodsucking she-devil? If the shoe fit…

"It's okay to have nice things," he told Lucy when she turned down his offer to buy her a fifty-dollar pair of sunglasses.

"I know, but I don't *need* them."

"So what? Why does everything have to be a debate? You like them, so just get them."

"It doesn't work like that for me. When I see something I like, I automatically tell myself all the reasons I don't need it, and I usually talk myself out of buying it."

Not this time. "Well, I'm getting them. Wear them, don't wear them, I don't care."

He grabbed the glasses from her and located the nearest register. Before she could catch up and stop him, the glasses were bought and paid for.

"See, that wasn't so bad," he said, handing her the bag. "Was it?"

Lucy cracked a smile. "I guess I'm just not used to someone wanting to do something nice for me."

"Then you had better get used to it. And you had better pick out some clothes, or I'm going to do it for you. And as you know, I'm about as fashion conscious as a house fly."

"The truth is, the clothes we've seen here aren't exactly my style," she admitted. "I know it's what's appropriate. But it's just not me."

He realized she was right. A lot of what they'd seen was stylish and chic, but geared more toward the career women, which for Lucy just wasn't all that practical. Screw appropriate, he just wanted her to be comfortable and happy. "Then we'll find something that's more you."

They came across an upscale boutique appropriately named Bun in the Oven, and the instant he saw the clothes in the window display, he knew they were in the right place. The outfits were young and hip, the fabrics soft and feminine.

As the stepped inside, Lucy gasped softly, gazing around in wonder. "I've never seen clothes so beautiful." She touched the silky sleeve of a peasant blouse, reaching for the tag to check the price.

"Don't even think about it," he said, taking her hand and holding it instead. "You're hereby forbidden to look at price tags."

A salesgirl greeted them warmly, her eyes lighting when Tony told her they would be purchasing an entire wardrobe. He'd never been one for clothes shopping. More often than not he called his tailor, told her what he needed and the items appeared magically a week or two later. It was a lot more fun buying clothes for someone else, watching Lucy twirl in front of the mirror as she tried on one outfit after another. He took a short break, leaving her in the salesgirl's capable hands, while he went in search of a jewelry store. When he returned, Lucy was still at it.

An hour later, they left the store with a half dozen huge bags containing all the clothes she would need to see her through the rest of her pregnancy. And after the baby was born, he intended to do this all over again. And hopefully next time they could do it without the argument.

"This is the nicest thing anyone has ever done for me," she told him, her eyes bright, her cheeks rosy with pleasure, like a child with a new toy.

"Get used to it," he told her.

She stopped at a bench outside the store and set down her bags, gesturing for him to do the same. Puzzled, he put the bags on the floor, and Lucy threw her arms around him. "Thank you so much."

"It was my pleasure," he said, holding her close. Speaking of pleasure...

The scent of her hair and her skin, her breath tickling his neck, her warm body pressed against him...it was all too much.

"Lucy," he said, his voice gravelly. He was going to pull away, he *needed* to, but then she looked up at him with those doe eyes of hers and all of his good intentions flew out the window.

Lucy whimpered softly as his lips covered hers, curling her fingers into the hair at his nape. Her lips were just as soft and delicious as he remembered.

For a few seconds he threw caution to the wind, allowed himself the pleasure of being close to her, and Lucy wasn't doing anything to stop him. In fact, she was kissing him deeper. If they were home, they would be halfway to his bedroom by now. But the sad fact was that they were in a public place, and by the time he got her to somewhere more private, she would have had time to change her mind.

It took every bit of strength that he possessed to pull away, but he did it.

"Wow," Lucy said breathlessly, stepping back, looking a little dazed and maybe a tiny bit scandalized. "You, uh, probably shouldn't do that again."

He was pretty sure he should, as soon as humanly possible.

"How about some lunch?" he said. Or a cold shower.

"Good idea. How about the food court?"

"Wouldn't you prefer to eat somewhere a little nicer?"

"Are you kidding?" she said, gathering up her bags. "I love the food court."

He shrugged. "The food court it is."

He got himself a burger and fries, she got a Caesar salad with double chicken and a loaded baked potato on the side. The seating area was packed with patrons but they found a two-person table by a window overlooking the Dumpsters.

"Charming view," Tony said, globbing ketchup onto his burger.

Lucy devoured her salad. "So don't look out the window."

To make up for it they would go someplace extra special for dinner. And maybe they could go see a movie. They used to do that a lot. Usually Sunday matinees, when admission was half price, because she always insisted she pay for her own ticket—though he would have been happy to do it.

"You want to catch dinner and a movie tonight?" he asked her. "There's a new Italian place downtown that sounds good."

"Actually, all the shopping we did knocked me on my butt. Why don't we order Chinese and stream a movie?"

"Are you sure?"

"Honestly, I'll be shocked if I make it past eight p.m."

"You have time to go home and catch a quick nap before I take you to *Nonno*'s."

"Ugh. I forgot about that. I don't think I could sleep."

"Just so you know, when I drop you at *Nonno*'s, I have some business to take care of at my lawyer's office. Just give me a call when you're ready to be picked up."

She was staring at him with an odd look on her face, her loaded fork hovering inches from her mouth. "When you *drop* me? Are you saying that you're not staying?"

He must have accidentally left that part out. "*Nonno* told me I couldn't come."

"So you're just going to leave me there?"

He didn't have much choice. "You'll be fine."

She didn't look convinced.

"Trust me."

She clearly did not. But she let it drop, though she seemed to suddenly lose interest in her food. "What kind of business do you have?"

"We have a conference call with a Realtor in Boca Raton."

That piqued her interest. "Are you buying another property?"

"I'm thinking about it. It would be my sixth place."

"That's awesome. You should do it."

"It just seems like a lot to take on with the baby coming. What started as a hobby is sucking up more and more of my time."

"But it's what you love to do."

She wasn't wrong about that. And it was a trade he'd fallen into accidentally. He had received bad advice and as a result lost more than half of his net worth when the economy tanked. Since then he'd been trying to rebuild his portfolio. He'd been looking for a low-risk, long-term investment. His lawyer had suggested he invest in a property. Like a summer home.

Being the director of overseas production and sales, he'd traveled all over the world. He spoke four different languages fluently, and could fumble his way through half a dozen others. He decided it would be fun to have a place somewhere foreign, and more importantly, *warm*. He chose Cabo. The problem was, he never had time to go there, and the upkeep was draining him. He started to think he'd fallen prey to more bad advice, until a friend suggested he rent it out during the periods of time he wasn't using it. It seemed like the perfect solution. It more than paid for the expenses of maintaining the property, and even brought him in a profit. When an opportunity rose to purchase another place for a steal, he took a leap of faith and it paid off. Then he bought another, then another, then a fifth property.

Currently he paid a management company to maintain the homes and find renters, but eventually he wanted to do it all himself. But that would be a full time position, and mean leaving Caroselli Chocolate. It would also mean plunking down a good chunk of cash as capital. Enter the thirty million from *Nonno.* He was so close he could almost feel the bills slide between his fingers, but he wasn't quite there yet. But if Lucy was wrong and they were having a girl...

His family was aware that he owned properties, but Lucy was the only person who knew of his aspirations in real estate.

Eventually he was going to make it work, though he was sure his family would freak out when he submitted his letter of resignation. The way he looked at it, he'd put in almost twenty years at a company he never wanted to work for in the first place. They owed him the opportunity to follow his own dreams. Now that he'd finally figured out what he wanted to do when he grew up. Better late than never.

If he hadn't taken his place at Caroselli Chocolate, Tony wasn't sure what he would have done after college. Or if he would have even gone to school. If it were up to him, he would have spent a year or two backpacking across Europe with a group of friends, but his father had absolutely forbade it, and like the good son that he'd always been, he'd obeyed. Sometimes he wondered how different his life would have been if he'd been more like his uncle Demitrio.

The way Tony's father told it, as a young boy Demitrio had been a troublemaker. The black sheep of the family, he had been intelligent, cocky and reckless—a dangerous combination. After one too many rides in the backseat of a police car, *Nonno* put his foot down. He gave Demitrio a choice. Join the army or go to jail and be disinherited. *Nonno* believed in tough love. Spare the rod, spoil the child.

It turned out to have been the best thing for Demitrio. After a stint in the army he went to university in France and graduated top of his class. After graduation he married his college sweetheart, Madeline, then moved back to the states and took his rightful place with Caroselli Chocolate, rapidly climbing the ranks. When *Nonno* had retired, he'd chosen Demitrio to take over as CEO, much to the chagrin of his two other sons.

Tony had asked his uncle once why he came back to Caroselli Chocolate when he could have done anything. Like Tony he was fluent in many languages, and had the financial means to live anywhere he wanted. Why stay here?

"Cut me and I bleed chocolate," Demitrio had said.

The only thing in Tony's veins was blood. The truth was, he didn't even like chocolate.

Lucy never thought she would find herself here again, standing on the porch of the Caroselli estate, knocking on the door. Though it had only been two days, in a way it felt like a lifetime ago. So much had happened since then. Nothing had gone the way she'd expected it to. All the plans she'd made, or had been trying to make, were now irrelevant.

As Tony had dropped her at the curb and driven away, she hadn't been able to shake the feeling that in order to appease his grandfather, he had served her up as sacrificial lamb. *Nonno* may have promised to be nice to her, but that didn't mean he would be. People as powerful as Guiseppe Caroselli didn't play by the same rules as everyone else. For all she knew, he could be planning to offer her a bribe to disappear. But for good this time.

Jeez, she was starting to think like her mom.

At least this time she was appropriately dressed for the occasion. She wasn't used to having nice things and she had been crazy careful all morning not to spill anything on herself. She'd even taken the time to put on eyeliner and lip gloss.

And unlike her previous visit, this time the door was answered by the butler. He wore a crisply pressed uniform slightly too large for him that seemed to pull his wiry shoulders forward and stoop his back. And he was *old.* As in, *Hey, what was it like to watch Moses part the Red Sea?* old. It was a wonder he was still able to work. Or still wanted to.

"I'm Lucy," she told him. "I'm here to see Mr. Caroselli."

With an arthritic dip of his head, he gestured her into the foyer. "He's expecting you. Please follow me."

She considered cracking a joke about missing him at the party Sunday, but he didn't strike her as the type to appreciate ironic humor. She followed him up the stairs… sloooowly…feeling a bit like a puppet whose strings were tangled, wrestling between frayed nerves, annoyance and wounded pride. Was she really going to let this man push her around? Let him intimidate her? But what would he do if she swung back?

The butler opened a door at the end of the hall. "Miss Lucy to see you, sir."

He gestured her through the door and she stepped into

the room—*Nonno*'s study. Tony told her that this was where *Nonno* conducted most of his business these days.

In his leather wingback chair, with a thick, hardback book resting on his spindly thighs, he looked so small and frail. So harmless. But she knew better. Tony had told her many times how ruthless he could be. How he ruled the family with an iron fist.

"Thank you, William," *Nonno* said, waving Lucy closer, peering at her over the top of a pair of round reading glasses. He assessed her from head to toe, his brow slightly furrowed as if he wasn't sure he liked what he was seeing.

"So this is the woman I've been hearing so much about." He spoke with a thick accent for someone who had been in the country for so many years.

"It's nice to meet you," she said, when in reality, she felt like she might barf.

"Come closer," he said. "Let me look at you."

She moved closer and tried not to flinch as he reached for her right hand, holding it between his two. His skin was cool and dry and so translucent she could see the network of bluish veins on the backs of his arthritic, age-spotted hands. He turned her hand over, looking first at the front, then the back, and he was kind enough not to mention her bitten down nails and ragged cuticles. What next? Her teeth? Her ears?

What was it that he saw when he looked at her?

"Interesting ring," he said, running his thumb over the greenish-blue stone set in braided silver.

"It's Ajax turquoise. It belonged to my grandmother. She was half Navajo."

"Yes," he said nodding absently, almost as if he already knew that. He ended the inspection there, letting go of her hand and gesturing to the sofa. "Sit, Lucy. Let's chat."

Would it be a chat, or an interrogation?

She sat, back straight, hands folded in her lap, bracing for the worst. And she got it.

"My grandson tells me that you refused to marry him."

Wow. He certainly got right to the point. And of course she immediately went on the defensive, though she couldn't deny it was a little refreshing to skip the small talk and get straight to the meat of the issue. Tony hadn't been exaggerating. *Nonno* may have been flirting with triple digits, but he was still sharp as a pin.

"That's right, I did. We don't have that kind of relationship."

"Friends with benefits, Tony called it."

Oh, my God. Had he actually told his grandfather that? Her cheeks burned with embarrassment. She wasn't sure how much of this she could take. She wanted Tony's family to accept her, but not at the expense of her pride. Or her feelings.

"Mr. Caroselli—"

"That's my great-grandchild you're carrying. You'll call me *Nonno*."

Ooookay. One second she's a slut, the next she's calling him Gramps? What kind of game was he playing?

"If I'm here so you can convince me that I'm not good enough for your grandson, why don't I save us both a very uncomfortable conversation? I am more than aware of the fact that Tony is too good for me. And despite what everyone thinks, I did not get pregnant on purpose, and I didn't come here to break up his wedding."

"Is that what everyone thinks?"

How could they not? "I have no illusions about who and what I am."

"And that's why you ran?" he asked.

Crap. He had to go and bring that up. "I didn't run. I *left.* There's a difference. I did what I thought was best for Tony. I knew he didn't want to settle down. Especially with someone like me."

"Or did you leave because you love him, and you were hoping he would follow?"

She tried, and failed, to hide her surprise. How could he possibly know that?

Regardless of how he knew, he seemed to be enjoying that he'd rattled her.

"If you want to know about love, it's the old men that you talk to," he said. "They know."

"Love has nothing to do with it."

"Young people," he said with a shake of his head, mumbling something in Italian.

"If you want to blame anyone for this situation, blame me," she told *Nonno.* "It's not Tony's fault."

"Tony is a good man," he said. "You'll never find anyone more loyal, or devoted to his family."

She waited for the inevitable warning. *Hurt him and I'll...*

It never came. For a long moment he just watched her. Then he said, "Do you cook, Lucy?"

Holy cow, he sure did switch gears fast. Or was this some sort of trick question? She wasn't good enough for his grandson if she couldn't prepare a decent meal? "Sort of. Does toast count?"

"Tony loves his *nonna*'s spaghetti sauce. You'll come over Friday and I'll teach you to make it."

Huh? Now he wanted to teach her to cook Tony's favorite food? These were not the actions of a man trying to get rid of someone. Maybe this was part of that promise he'd made Tony. Maybe he felt obligated to be nice to her.

"I…sure, if it's not too much trouble."

"Come at one p.m. sharp."

"Okay."

Nonno turned and looked out the window, then sighed deeply and closed his eyes, which she took to mean conversation over. No wasted words with this man. He said what he wanted to say, and when he was done, he was done. She respected that.

She quietly let herself out of the study, thinking how that wasn't nearly as bad as she'd expected. In fact, it hadn't been bad at all. She was almost looking forward to coming back on Friday. It's not as if she had anything better to do, and she'd always wanted to learn how to cook. It would probably be fun if she had all the necessary elements. Like, say, ingredients.

Maybe she was being overly optimistic, or fooling herself—she was really good at that—but she had the feeling that maybe, just maybe, *Nonno* thought she might not be so bad.

But when all was said and done, she walked away from the conversation more confused than when she got there.

Seven

Tony watched the monitor with fascination as the ultrasound tech probed Lucy's stomach, poking and prodding, going from one side back to the other through a puddle of bluish goo. He knew the 4D ultrasound showed a lot of detail, but he hadn't expected to be able to see the baby in real time, kicking his legs, sucking his thumb. He even yawned.

Tony could even see that he had the Caroselli nose, and Lucy's ears, and considering he only had two and a half more months to cook, he didn't look all that small.

"Would you like to know the sex of the baby?" the tech asked them.

"Yes," Tony told her, and Lucy quickly countered with, "We absolutely do not."

They had debated all last evening, and this morning before her appointment. Did they want to know or didn't they? For obvious reasons Tony wanted to know sooner rather than later.

"I want to be surprised," she told the technician, and said to Tony, "If you know, you'll want to tell me."

"No, I won't," Tony said.

"Yes, you will."

No, he wouldn't. "Have a little faith."

"I have to take measurements and in just a minute or two the gender is going to be very obvious," the technician said, looking a little exasperated by their bickering. But it probably wasn't the first time she had heard that argument between expecting parents. "Here we go. If you don't want to know, don't look at the screen."

"Look away," Lucy ordered, turning her face to the wall and closing her eyes, and he dutifully turned with her.

"I'll let you know when it's safe to look," the technician told them, and Tony glanced over his shoulder at the screen, but what caught his attention first was the furrowed brow of the tech. Was she just concentrating, or did she see something wrong? He looked past her to the screen and...*hello*. When she said the gender would be obvious she wasn't kidding. He turned away, but he couldn't contain the smile tugging at his lips. The mystery was over. And suddenly this becoming a father thing seemed very real in a way he hadn't been able to comprehend when they stepped into the room. It was one thing to know there was a baby, but to see it on the screen, especially in so much detail, took it to a whole new level.

He was going to be a father. He was going to be responsible for the care and feeding of that tiny, helpless little person. That should have scared the hell out of him, but he felt an unprecedented sensation of well-being, of pure calm. He had always said he wanted kids someday, but he never truly understood how much. Or what that would mean.

He was ready for this. And those three months they had to wait for the birth sounded like an eternity to him.

"All done," the technician said, handing Lucy a wad of tissues to clean up the goo, and ejecting a disk from the unit. "I'll be back in a minute."

He took Lucy's hand and helped her sit up.

"That was fun," she said. "I had no idea that the picture would be that clear."

"Me neither. I think he has my nose."

"And my elephant ears."

He grinned and rubbed her left earlobe between his fingers. "I like your elephant ears."

She smiled up at him and his eyes snagged on hers. A look passed between them. One that said maybe they should *stop* looking.

Maybe it was odd, but he found her just as attractive, or maybe even more attractive, pregnant. He wondered if the sex would have been different somehow. Would he have to be gentler? She'd never been one to hold back in bed.

"I have something for you," he said, pulling the small velvet box from his jacket pocket. "I was going to wait until later, but I think you should have this now." It would take his mind off of getting her naked.

Her eyes went a little wide when she saw the box and she sucked in a quiet breath. "What did you do?"

"Well, I was thinking about diamonds," he said, casually tossing the box from one hand to the other. "But then I thought, nah, Lucy is too unique for plain old diamonds."

"You think I'm unique?"

"I do. In a *good* way."

She smiled. "I knew what you meant."

He handed her the box. "The instant I saw these I knew I had to get them for you."

She opened it very slowly, as if she expected something to jump out at her. When her gaze focused on the earrings set in a bed of white satin, she gasped.

"Ajax turquoise, the same stone as my ring! I love them!"

She must have, because she put them on immediately. With her dark hair and eyes and olive skin, the blue in the stones really popped.

"Beautiful," he said with a grin, and he didn't mean the jewelry. They had another one of those gaze-locking encounters, and for a second it felt as if the room shifted beneath his feet, then he realized he was the one moving, leaning in. Her tongue darted out to wet her lips, as if she were anticipating his kiss. Then the tech walked back in and killed the moment.

"I'll thank you later," she said softly, and he really hoped she meant what he thought she did.

"Can I have you two sit in the waiting room?" the tech asked.

His heart bottomed out and the color drained from Lucy's face. "Is there a problem?"

"Dr. Hannan just needs a minute to look over the scan. They'll let you know if he needs to see you."

She showed them to the waiting room, which was blessedly empty, and they took a seat in the corner. He could see that Lucy was nervous, and that made him nervous.

"Do you get the feeling something is wrong?" she asked him, their brief interlude long forgotten.

"I'm sure they're just being extra careful, with the baby being small." It was a lie. He'd seen the look on the tech's face. Now he was more convinced than ever that she saw something she didn't like.

"He doesn't feel very small," she said, shifting in her seat to get comfortable, hands resting on the top of her belly.

"I'm no expert, but he didn't look very small to me, either."

"Are you sorry that we didn't learn the sex of the baby?"

He shrugged. "Hmm."

She blinked. "What does that mean?"

"It means hmm."

She drew in a sharp breath. "*You peeked,* didn't you? You looked at the screen."

"Why would I do that?"

"Don't even try to lie to me. You looked. Admit it."

He just smiled.

"But we agreed!"

"No, we didn't," he said. "I never agreed to anything."

"Don't you *dare* tell me."

"So I should forget that announcement in the *Tribune?*"

Her exasperated expression made him smile. "I really don't want to know," she said.

"I won't say a word. To anyone."

"You promise?"

"Even if you beg and plead with me, I will not tell you. I promise."

She narrowed her eyes at him, trying to appear stern, but just under the surface she was smiling.

The door to the reception area opened and they both tensed as a nurse leaned out. "Ms. Bates, Dr. Hannan will see you now."

Lucy mumbled a curse under her breath. A heavy-duty expletive that, as far as he could recall, he'd never heard her use before.

He reached for her hand, weaving his fingers through hers. She clung to him as the nurse led them to an exam room.

"He'll be right with you," she said, closing the door when she left.

"This is my fault," Lucy said as he helped her up onto the exam table. She was holding his hand so tight he was losing the feeling in his fingers.

"We don't even know if anything is wrong." And if there was, it could be something genetic from his side, something she had no control over. Other than to not get pregnant in the first place.

"If nothing was wrong we wouldn't be here," Lucy said.

"That's not necessarily true." Though he had been thinking the same thing. The fear that it might be something really bad was tying his stomach in knots, but he refused to let it show. She needed to know that he would always remain strong for her. A few days ago he didn't even know about the baby, and now, he would move heaven and earth to see that he was healthy. Whatever it took.

They sat there for nearly twenty minutes stewing in their anxiety, making idle chitchat to kill the time but not actually saying anything of substance or significance. When the doctor finally opened the door Lucy was wound so tight, she nearly launched off the table.

"Sorry to keep you waiting," Dr. Hannan said, closing the door behind him.

"Is anything wrong?" Lucy asked, as he rechecked her blood pressure.

"Do you tend to get nervous at the doctor's office? Your pressure is a little high today."

"I hate going to the doctor."

"I'm going to have the nurse draw another blood sample," Dr. Hannan said. "I'd like to do a few additional tests." He listened to her heart, then her lungs. "Until we get the results, try to stay off your feet if you can. I'd like you to rest as much as possible."

"Are you putting me on bed rest?"

"No, but I do want you to take it easy. If you're doing something that keeps you on your feet for an extended amount of time, take a break every hour or so and put them up for a few minutes."

"Okay," she said, and Tony knew exactly what she was thinking. She was not an idle person. That was going to be a tough one for her to stick to.

"I'm going to have the nurse draw another blood sample," Dr. Hannan said. "I'd like to do a few additional tests."

"Should we be worried?" Tony asked him, wondering just how serious this was. Staying off her feet was one thing, but more tests? That didn't sound good.

"It's probably nothing," he assured them. "I just want to be sure that we cover all of our bases. I'll see that they rush the results. I should have a report back tomorrow. Friday at the latest."

They might have to wait two days? He and Lucy would be basket cases by then.

"What about the ultrasound?" Lucy said. "Was everything okay?"

"Just to be thorough I'm going to have a colleague look over the scan, but on the surface everything seemed pretty good. The baby's size could be an issue, but I believe that adequate nutrition will be the key to getting you and the baby to a healthy weight."

He made a few notes on her chart, and then the nurse came in and took three more vials of her blood. Leave some for the baby, Tony wanted to say. Lucy's face was so pale, she already looked anemic. Having just come back from four months in Florida, she should have had a tan, right? Or maybe she hadn't gotten out much.

For most of the drive home she sat beside him, absently sliding her hand back and forth over her belly. He put the radio on to fill the bubble of silence growing ever more conspicuous between them, and even chose a station that played the bass thumping techno dance stuff she liked to listen to. Two minutes later it started to feel as if someone had shoved a knitting needle through his temple.

Lucy reached over and shut the radio off. "What if something really is wrong?"

Then they would deal with it. Whatever it was. "Like the doctor said, there's no point worrying until there's something to worry about."

"That's easy for you to say."

"No," he glanced over at her, "it's not. I'm worried, too."

"I'm sorry," she said. "That was unfair. Of course you are."

"You know what might make things easier?"

"What?"

"If you married me."

She shot him a look.

That was a definite no. "No matter what it is, if it's anything at all, we'll deal with it. Together. Everything will be okay."

"You're right," she said, with a smile that was almost genuine. "I have to be positive."

He was glad she believed him. Now, if he could just manage to convince himself.

When *Nonno* said he would teach her to make the sauce, Lucy had assumed he would make it and she would watch. She was wrong. He claimed that doing all the work was part of the learning process. She sort of had the feeling his cook had the day off and Lucy was just a hapless replacement.

Though she had still been apprehensive about coming here, it sure beat sitting home, twiddling her thumbs, wondering what was wrong with the baby. Or her. Or worse, both of them. Tony must have felt the same way, because instead of going back home after he dropped her at *Nonno*'s, he went into the office instead, even though he'd sworn he was taking the rest of the week off. Honestly, she couldn't blame him.

First, *Nonno* had her gather all the ingredients from the pantry and refrigerator, along with a big silver pot from the cupboard that had seen its fair share of time on an open flame.

He sat on a stool at the kitchen island, taking her through the steps of the recipe, telling her to add a pinch of this and a touch of that. He never once had her use a measuring spoon.

"This isn't so hard," she said, wiping her hands on the apron he'd given her to wear. She stirred the contents of the pot with a wooden spoon. "And it smells delicious."

"I think you're a natural."

"It's fun. Though I'm not sure I'll remember all that."

"Don't worry, I'll write it down for you."

"With actual measurements?"

"Yes, yes, with measurements."

"I'll add it to my journal so I'll always have it."

"My Angelica kept a journal," *Nonno* said. "I buried it with her. My children were not happy with me."

"They wanted to read it?"

"Yes, but they were Angelica's private thoughts, and no one else's business. Including mine."

"My journal is online, so no one without a password can access it. It started out as a school project, but I liked it so much I kept writing."

He patted the stool beside him. "Come, sit with me."

She wondered if Tony had told him what the doctor said about her staying off her feet. After sitting idle for two days, it felt good to move around, to get out of the apartment. If the doctor were to ever put her on total bed rest, she would need a padded room within the first week.

"Sit. Rest," *Nonno* said. "Soon we'll start the noodles."

Even *she* could boil noodles.

She rinsed her hands at the sink then sat down beside him. "How did you learn to cook?"

"My *madre*. She was a cook for a wealthy family in our village. She also made candy and sold it to the local merchants. I helped her."

"What did your father do?"

"He was a merchant. But he died when I was very small."

"Was it just you and your mom?"

"Yes, just the two of us. We had very little. Many nights we went to bed hungry."

That certainly was something they had in common.

"You, too," he said, and it wasn't a question. He already knew.

"Tony told you?"

"I could see it in your eyes." He laid a hand over hers and patted gently, and something about the gesture made her want to cry. He was being so kind to her. Despite who she was.

"My mom and I didn't have much, either," she told him. "And it was just the two of us."

"I helped as much as a child could. When I was old enough, I sold our candy from a cart on the street, going door to door, every single day, until the cart was empty. That's how I met my Angelica."

"Was it love at first sight?" she asked him.

"It was for me. But she was from a wealthy family and her parents did not want a peddler for a son-in-law."

"Did you elope?"

"We planned to, but her parents found out and took her away. To America."

Wow, talk about harsh. Moving their daughter halfway around the world to get him out of her life. "So what did you do?"

"I followed her."

"Here? To Chicago."

He nodded, the memory making him smile, lighting his face with a youthful glow.

Memories were powerful things.

"She was the love of my life. My other half. I would move heaven and earth to be with her."

It sounded as if he had.

"We began to meet in secret, but soon her father found out."

"What did he do?"

"When he realized that I would not give up so easily, he made me a deal. I could have his daughter's hand when I could provide for her in a manner he saw fit. No easy task for a young man selling chocolate, I assure you. The day I opened the doors to the first Caroselli Chocolate store in downtown Chicago, I asked again. This time he called me foolish and said I would fail. That I would never amount to anything, and I would never be good enough for his daughter. A year later I owned three stores and still couldn't keep up with demand. So I asked him again."

"And?"

Nonno smiled. "He gave us his blessing."

Lucy dropped her chin in her palm and sighed wistfully. "I think that's the most romantic story I've ever heard." Tony had told her that his grandfather came to this country with only twenty dollars in his pocket, but she hadn't realized how poor he had actually been, and what hard work it must have taken to build his fortune.

For some reason the idea made him seem a little less intimidating.

"Could you imagine how different my life would have been if I had listened to him? If I had believed I wasn't good enough. Instead, every time he doubted my worthiness, I worked that much harder to prove him wrong. I think he meant it to happen exactly that way. If not for my father-in-law, I would not be the success I am today."

He was lucky to have someone who saw his potential, someone who cared enough to push him in the right direction.

"Now, for the noodles," he said, rubbing his hands together in anticipation. "We'll need flour and eggs."

Flour and eggs? Why would they need that to boil noodles?

"And in the pantry on the top shelf you'll find the pasta maker."

Wait a minute. *Pasta maker?* "Are we actually *making* the noodles? Like, from scratch?"

"My mother's recipe," he said, tapping his temple. "It's all up here."

Her first thought was, so much for this being easy. But then they got started and she realized it wasn't really all that complicated. *Nonno* showed her how to make a crater in the center of the flour, then add the wet ingredients and fold it in on itself, over and over until it was thoroughly mixed. It was fun running the dough through the rollers, watching it grow thinner and thinner until it was ready to cut into strips, which they left to dry on racks.

When they were finished she got up from the stool and gave the sauce a stir. It really did smell amazing.

Her stomach growled greedily. So loudly that *Nonno* heard it.

"Ah," he said with a smile, one that crinkled his eyes, and showed off teeth that may not have been perfect, but were his own. "You approve."

"I can't wait to try it. Although I think we made enough to feed an army."

"We do have many people to feed tonight."

Her hand stopped mid-stir. Did he say tonight? As in *tonight?*

"What people?"

"The family, of course."

Eight

"They come the last Friday of every month," *Nonno* told Lucy.

And it was indeed the last Friday of the month. Her heart sank. "So, I'm making dinner for your entire family?"

Nonno nodded.

Aw, hell. She knew Tony ate at his grandfather's the last Friday of every month, but she hadn't made the connection.

Suddenly she wasn't all that hungry anymore. Even worse, what food she did have in her stomach wanted to come back up for a visit.

"I need to rest," *Nonno* said, rising slowly from the stool, appearing a little unsteady on his feet. "When I wake up, we'll do the salad."

Meaning he expected her to stay. Well, crap. What was she supposed to do now? He'd been so nice to her today. It would be rude not to stick around, but to meet the entire enormous family in *one* night? Why didn't he just toss her into a cage with a pack of hungry wolves, or a tank of bloodthirsty piranha?

Either way she would be ripped to shreds.

"Walk with me," *Nonno* said, taking her arm to steady himself. As they walked slowly through the kitchen to the elevator, she thought about his story, and the way he'd followed his beloved Angelica around the world. It tugged at her heartstrings, and at the same time made her inexplicably sad. She could only wish that someday someone would love her so completely that he would move heaven and earth to be with her.

"You were right," she said, the words coming out of her mouth before she had even decided to say them. "I left hoping that Tony would follow me. He didn't."

It stung to admit that. To leave herself so vulnerable. For the first time in her life she had let herself wish for something. Something big. Unconditional love.

She should have known better.

Nonno gave her arm a reassuring squeeze as they stepped in the elevator and the doors rolled closed.

"I wasn't supposed to fall in love with him," she said, feeling as if she should explain. So he would understand why someone like her would get her hopes up about a guy like his grandson. "I didn't think I even knew how to love someone. Then bam, there it was. And he didn't love me back. How's that for irony."

"You told him this? That you love him?"

"Absolutely not. It would be too humiliating."

He looked confused. "Because you assume that he doesn't love you?"

"It seems like a pretty safe bet."

"Ah, but mind reading is tricky business."

"Mind reading?"

"Isn't that what you're doing? How can Tony know how you feel if you don't tell him?"

Because what she felt didn't matter. "Didn't Tony tell you that he and I are just friends with benefits? It doesn't get much clearer than that. That's all it ever was to him. All it was ever *supposed* to be. It's not his fault that I blew it. That *I* broke the rules."

"But your feelings changed. Couldn't they could have changed for him as well?"

Why was he pushing so hard about this? "Did Tony say something to you?"

A vague smile pulled at his tired eyes. "Tony says many things to me."

She wasn't sure how to take that. The door opened and he let go of her arm to step off the elevator. She expected him to turn and say something else, but he walked into his room directly across the hall and closed the door.

What the heck had he been trying to say to her?

She took the stairs down, calling Tony to see if he could drive her home to change. In black leggings and a long sweater, she wasn't exactly dressed for dinner. He didn't answer, so she left a message. She hoped it was casual Friday.

She stepped back into the kitchen, and was startled by the male figure hunched over the pot of sauce until she realized it was Tony. He had incredible timing.

"Hey, I just called you," she said.

He turned, rising to his full height, and only then did she notice the gray feathered through the man's dark hair.

"I'm sorry," she said, her cheeks flaming with embarrassment. "I thought you were Tony."

"Demitrio," he said. "Tony's uncle."

So this was the CEO of Caroselli Chocolate. She'd expected someone much more…something. Intimidating maybe. But in jeans and a polo shirt, he just seemed like a regular guy.

"You must be Lucy," he said.

She accepted his outstretched hand. It was eerie how

alike he and Tony not only looked but sounded. If she closed her eyes and listened to each of them, she might have a hard time telling them apart.

She could only imagine the things going through his head at that moment, like, what was this stranger doing snooping around his father's house? "You're probably wondering what I'm doing here," she said.

He smiled. The same quirky, slightly lopsided grin that she had seen on Tony a bazillion times. "The tomato-stained apron sort of speaks for itself."

"Oh, right." She'd forgotten she was wearing it. "Cooking lesson."

"I figured. Is *Nonno* around?"

"He just laid down for a nap."

"My contribution to dinner," Demitrio said, gesturing to a bakery bag stuffed with long thin loaves of unsliced bread that he'd left on the table. "I might be a little late tonight, so I thought it best to bring it by now."

"I'm sure he'll appreciate that."

Demetrio flashed her a smile that was so Tony, it gave her a bizarre little shiver. She must have been looking at him funny, because he asked her, "Everything all right?"

She shook the fog from her brain. She was making an even bigger fool of herself than usual. "Yes, sorry. I don't mean to stare. It's just that you and Tony look so much alike. You even sound alike."

His grin was a wry one. "It's almost as if we're related."

They had the same ironic sense of humor as well, and there was something about Demitrio that put her at ease. Just the way Tony had when they first met.

That was three people in the family who didn't seem to hate her guts. Four including Tony. Only a couple dozen to go.

"Helloooo! Lucy?" someone called, and they both turned to see Tony's mom glide into the room. She smiled when she saw Lucy standing there, but when she noticed Demitrio, she stopped abruptly and the smile disappeared. "Oh. Hello, Demitrio."

"Sarah," he said, nodding cordially, his expression tight. "I was just on my way out."

Whoa, talk about tension. They were definitely not happy to see each other.

"It was nice to meet you, Lucy," Demitrio said.

"You, too. I'll see you later."

When he was gone, Sarah turned to her and smiled, but Lucy could see that she was shaken by the encounter. Of course she wondered why, but it was *so* not any of her business.

"I came by to make sure *Nonno* wasn't wearing you out," Sarah said. "Tony told me what the doctor said about keeping off your feet."

"He did?" Hadn't they agreed not to say anything to the family until they heard back about her test results?

"For the record, Tony didn't voluntarily tell me about the appointment. I had lunch with Gina yesterday and she mentioned that Nick and Terri saw you two at Dr. Hannan's office. I browbeat the details out of him."

"Gina?"

"My sister-in-law. Nick's mom. Who technically isn't my sister-in-law since she divorced Leo, my brother-in-law. But they just set a date."

"Set a date?"

"For their wedding."

"They're getting married again?"

She shrugged, as if she didn't understand it, either. "I'll believe it when I see it. I love Gina like a sister, but she's always been a little…well, flaky. But who am I to pass judgment?"

Weirder things had happened.

"Enough about my crazy relatives," she said, waving the subject away like a pesky insect. "How do you feel?"

"Physically I feel fine. It's hard to imagine that something could be wrong."

"So you haven't heard from the doctor?"

"Not yet. He said Friday at the latest."

"Well, try not to worry. My instincts are telling me that everything will be just fine. I have a sixth sense about these things."

She hoped Sarah was right. In Lucy's experience, if something had the potential to go badly, it usually did. She just couldn't seem to shake the feeling that something was terribly wrong with the baby. And it was her fault. She had never been particularly religious, but if there was a God, she hoped He would cut her a break this time.

"Have you started making a list of the things you'll need?" Sarah asked.

"Things?"

"For the baby. Three months probably seems like a long time, but take it from someone who's been there, the days will fly by. It's good to be prepared."

"I guess I need everything. But maybe we should wait until we hear from the doctor. I would hate to spend a lot of money on a bunch of baby stuff we'll never use."

"Oh, Lucy," Sarah said, and then she did something totally unexpected. She pulled Lucy into her arms and hugged her hard. Lucy was so stunned by the gesture, she wasn't sure how to react. She couldn't even recall her own mom ever holding her this way, much less a practical stranger. With so much compassion, and genuine affection.

Something deep inside of Lucy urged her to pull away, to keep her distance, but she was so tired of being alone. So tired of constantly pushing everyone away. So she didn't. She took a huge leap of faith, hugging Sarah back, dissolving into a sobbing, sniffling blob. And once she got started, she couldn't seem to stop."

"Oh, honey, it'll be okay," Sarah said, rubbing her back soothingly. Like a real mom. The kind who actually gave a damn about someone other than herself. "You just let it out."

Knowing she was making a huge fool of herself, but helpless to stop it, Lucy was glad that no one else was around to see her meltdown—

"What did I miss?" someone said from behind them. A female voice with a distinct French accent.

Oh, hell.

Lucy sniffled and opened her eyes. Standing in the kitchen doorway was a tall, leggy blonde who, despite being Sarah's age at least, looked young and stylish in a cream cashmere sweater and jeggings, her hair pulled back in a sleek ponytail. But when she saw the tears still clinging to Lucy's cheeks, her smile dissolved and she dropped her purse on the counter. "Oh, Jesus, who died?"

"Tony! Wake up?"

Tony bolted up in his chair, blinking himself awake, disoriented until he realized that he was still at the office.

"Are you going to *Nonno*'s?"

He looked up and saw his uncle Demitrio standing in his office doorway. He looked out the window; it was growing dark outside. How long had he been sleeping? "Yeah, of course. I'll be there."

"Give an old man a lift? Your Aunt Madeline has my car."

"Sure," he said, rubbing his eyes. "What time is it?"

Demitrio looked at his watch. "Six-thirty."

"*Six-thirty?*" With a curse, he shot to his feet. He vaguely remembered leaning back in his chair and closing his eyes, thinking a twenty-minute nap would probably do him good. That was two and a half *hours* ago. Lucy was going to kill him. She was probably sitting in a corner at *Nonno*'s plotting a very slow and painful death at that very moment.

"Oversleep?" Demitrio asked, looking mildly amused.

Oh, had he ever.

"I haven't been getting much sleep since Lucy has been back."

His uncle grinned and Tony realized he'd taken that the wrong way. "What I mean is, I've given Lucy my bed and I'm sleeping on the fold-out couch in my office. It's about as comfortable as a medieval torture device."

"So you two aren't...?"

"Truth is, I'm not exactly sure what we are." He rose from his chair. "You ready to go?"

Demitrio shrugged. "Sure."

Tony grabbed his jacket, tugging it on as they headed for the elevator.

"I sense some urgency to get there quickly," his uncle said.

"I had planned to get to *Nonno*'s early so I could be there when Lucy met everyone. She doesn't really have any family, and you know that ours can be a little intimidating at first."

Demitrio laughed. "That's putting it mildly."

They stepped into the elevator and rode it down to the parking garage. "They'll eat her alive."

"I don't know about that. I met Lucy today when I

stopped by *Nonno*'s. She strikes me as the type of girl who can hold her own."

"Oh, she is, but it would be nice if she didn't have to for a change."

Traffic was heavy, and by the time they made it to *Nonno*'s everyone had started without them. Dinner was at seven sharp. It had been that way Tony's entire life. Show up on time or eat your food cold…if there was any left. This was the one day out of the month that everyone threw caution to the wind and blew their diet. It was a feast, really.

He spotted Lucy in the first chair next to *Nonno,* who always sat at the head of the table. Seated to her left was his mom, and beside her, his dad. Lucy was having what looked like a very animated conversation with the three of them. And she was smiling. But there was something different about her smile this time. Why had he never noticed the way it lit her entire face?

He had the strongest urge to walk over to her chair, pull her to her feet and just hold her. Even if his entire family was watching. At the moment he didn't care who saw them. He just wanted to touch her. And he wanted to apologize for being so damned inconsiderate. It would serve him right if she clocked him.

"You're late," *Nonno* told them, alerting everybody at the table who hadn't seen Tony and his uncle come in. Like Lucy.

She turned and saw him standing there. He waited for the smile to fade, but it only grew wider. Was it possible that she was happy to see him?

"Sit," *Nonno* ordered.

Aunt Madeline had saved his uncle a seat, so Tony took the only other empty chair, which was next to Nick at the opposite end of the table from Lucy. As the serving plates made the rounds he dutifully filled his plate, but he had a tough time keeping his eyes off Lucy. There was something distinctly different about her. Her skin glowed and her eyes sparkled. It was as if she'd come alive since he dropped her at *Nonno*'s house that afternoon. Or maybe it was his perception that had changed?

Lucy didn't like to talk about her family and he was sure there was a good reason for that. Maybe her childhood was worse than he'd imagined. Could it be that this was the first time he'd seen her smile and really mean it?

The thought gave him a knot in his throat.

Christ, what was wrong with him? What was with this sudden feeling of protectiveness, of wanting to take care of her? He'd never experienced anything like it. He only knew that he would do practically anything to keep her safe. To make her happy.

When he thought about losing her…

The air backed up in his lungs. Nope, he couldn't go through that again.

"Lucy looks good," Nick said when he passed Tony the carrots. Tony took some, even though he didn't have much of an appetite. "Everyone likes her and is wondering why this is the first time they're meeting her."

And they would have to keep wondering because it was none of their business.

"You dated her for like, what? A year?"

"Almost." If you could even call it dating. They were just…having fun. And if Nick was expecting details he would be thoroughly disappointed. Thankfully he had the attention span of a fruit fly, so Tony had no problem steering him away to a different subject. There was nothing Nick loved more than talking about himself.

"Hey, how did the ultrasound go?" Tony asked him. "Did you find out what you're having?"

"That's right, you missed it," he said with a grin.

"Missed what," Tony asked.

"Our announcement tonight. Terri wanted to do it that way. With flair."

"Jesus, she's really turning into one of us, isn't she?"

"Scary, I know."

"I heard that," Terri said from two seats over, giving her husband a look.

Nick winked and blew her a kiss and the look dissolved into a smile.

"It's a girl," she told Tony.

"Wow, congratulations!"

"How is Lucy doing with her pregnancy?" Terri asked him.

"For about a month Terri was pretty miserable with morning sickness," Nick said. "Which never seemed to happen in the morning, oddly enough. There was no predicting it. Out of the blue she would get this look, and God help us if we weren't near a bathroom. It's amazing the creative places you can find to barf when you're really desperate."

From the other side of Nick, his sister Jessica leaned over and said, "Hey moron. Can we please talk about something other than *barfing* while we're eating dinner?"

"Yeah, sorry," Tony said, giving Nick a shove.

"Thank God that's over now," Nick said. "The whole first three months kind of sucked if you ask me."

He wouldn't know. "I missed that part."

"Well, consider yourself lucky."

Tony wasn't feeling all that lucky. Instead, he was feeling like he'd made a huge mistake.

It must have shown on his face.

Nick set his fork down. "Tony, I'm really sorry. That was an insensitive thing to say."

Tony shrugged. "Don't worry about it."

"You want to take a swing at me?"

Tony laughed. "That's okay. I appreciate the offer, though."

"You know, there's something different about you lately," Nick said.

"It's not every week a man learns his ex is pregnant with his child."

"No," Nick said. "This started a while ago. Before Alice, even. In fact, I started to notice a change right around the time Lucy left."

After she left, he kept waiting to feel like himself again. The way he felt before he met Lucy. But he was beginning to believe that the man he was before Lucy simply didn't exist anymore. Meeting her had changed him. He hadn't even realized it until she was no longer there. "I guess her leaving hit me harder than I wanted to admit."

"Love is a funny thing. Terri and I were friends for almost twenty years before we figured out that we're supposed to be together. If it hadn't been for *Nonno* and his bribe, we might have gone through life never making that connection."

Is that what was happening to him? Was he falling in love with Lucy? Or was it possible that he was already there? Technically he had never been in love—at least, not that he knew of—so how was he supposed to know what it felt like?

Dinner seemed to drag on forever, then Lucy helped clear the table which took another ten minutes. Then his dad and his Uncle Leo roped him into a conversation about work. Chocolate, his least favorite subject lately. When he was able to break free, he went looking for Lucy and found her sitting on the sofa surrounded by children.

She looked up, saw him standing there and smiled. With a jerk of his head he gestured for her to follow him. But as she was getting up his sister Alana intercepted her.

He was happy that she was getting along with everyone, but come on. This is why he never brought women to meet his family. They sucked people in. Whether they wanted to be sucked in or not. That used to annoy the hell out him, but now he was grateful. They may have been loud and obnoxious and nosy, but they really did mean well. He'd never truly appreciated that before now.

But enough already.

He walked over to where she and his sister stood. "Can I borrow Lucy?"

"Nice of you to show up," Alana said. "If I were Lucy, I wouldn't marry you, either."

Seriously? His family was on Lucy's side? "And everyone wonders why I never bring a guest to dinner," he said, taking Lucy's hand and pulling her along with him.

"Where are we going?" she asked.

"Someplace we can be alone." He led her upstairs to the spare bedroom, which he knew had a lock on the door, and he used it. Then he took her by the shoulders and turned her to face him, taking it all in. "Wow."

She looked down at herself, then back up to him. "I know, I'm enormous."

"No. You look beautiful."

"Oh, it's the dress," she said, smoothing the silky material over her belly.

Honestly, he hadn't even noticed what she was wearing, but now that he had, he liked it. It was…the icing on the cake. She could wear a burlap sack and he would still want her. "It isn't the dress. It's you."

She flushed with pleasure.

"I'm *so* sorry. I wanted to be here when you met everyone."

"It's okay."

He shook his head. "No, it's not."

"It *really* is. I mean, like, I should be thanking you. It was good for me to do this alone. I'm glad that I didn't know about dinner when you dropped me off. I probably would have found some excuse to get out of it."

"What do you mean, you didn't know about dinner? It's the last Friday of the month."

"I know. I guess I forgot. We've both been preoccupied lately."

That was an understatement. "I should have thought to remind you," he said.

"It's not your fault."

No, it was. She needed him to be on top of things, to take care of her. "Lucy, I'm sorry. I guess…I've been having dinner at my grandparents' house every last Friday of every month for most of my life. I don't even consciously show up. I get in the car after work and it just drives itself here."

"Like I said, it's okay. I had *so* much fun today. *Nonno* isn't at all like I expected. No one was."

"What did you expect?"

She hesitated. "Well, you didn't paint a very pretty picture of your family, so…"

"I didn't?"

"In a year I barely heard you say a positive word about any of them."

No, that couldn't be right. Was he really that negative when he talked about his family?

"And who is Carrie?"

"Rob's wife. I didn't see her here."

"I guess she's in Los Angeles. Everyone keeps asking if I met her yet. I'm assuming there's a reason why."

Yep, there was. "Alice is her best friend."

"*Oooooh*. Now I get it."

"That's how I met Alice."

"Carrie is going to hate me, isn't she?"

He shook his head. "Not if she takes the time to get to know you."

"You think so?"

"I do." Lucy was so nice, so easy to get along with, he couldn't imagine anyone not liking her. Besides, she had nothing to do with his relationship with Alice. That was all on him.

"I know you almost just got here, but would you mind if we went home?" Lucy asked. "Or maybe you could drop me home and come back? I'm beyond exhausted."

"You were supposed to be resting today."

"And I did, just like Dr. Hannan said. I think all this waiting around is starting to get to me."

"I guess that means you haven't heard from the doctor."

She shook her head. "I really hoped we would hear today, but what are the chances he'd call on a Friday night?"

She had a point. So they would have to wait until Monday, which meant it was going to be a very *long* weekend.

It was eight-thirty when they decided to leave *Nonno*'s house, and almost nine by the time they made it to the car. Lucy never knew it could take so long to say goodbye. In one day, she hadn't received so many hugs and kisses since…well, probably ever. She didn't think there was a single shy or reserved individual among the Carosellis. She had been worried she would wind up sitting in the corner bored while the family did their thing. She should have listened when Tony told her that they sucked people in. He was right. She had always thought that sounded sort of creepy. But it wasn't, not at all. It almost felt as if she had a real family.

They were loud, they were nosy, and they were *wonderful*.

"So, I guess that's what's it like to be in a big family," she said.

Tony chuckled. "A certifiably crazy family."

"But you wouldn't trade them in for anything."

"I don't know. I might be willing to negotiate." He glanced over at her, grinning. "What are you offering?"

"Be careful what you wish for." She would take them in a minute. She sure wished someone would take her mom off her hands.

"Maybe I wouldn't trade them," he said, "but I might be willing to loan them out."

A loaner family? Wasn't that better than no family at all? "Your mom was so amazing to me today, and I really liked your uncle Demitrio."

"Yeah. I love my uncle Leo, but Demitrio and I have always been closer for some reason."

"You look just like him."

"Do I?"

He hadn't noticed? Had the man never looked in a mirror? "You look alike, and sound alike. You even laugh alike. And you have the same build. When I first saw him I thought it was you."

"I guess we do look a little alike," he said.

"Do he and your mom not like each other? When she walked in, there was tension."

"Old scars maybe. I don't know. My dad and Demitrio got into it a couple of months ago."

"An argument?"

"More like a brawl."

"Seriously?"

"Leo had to pull them apart. I'm assuming that it has something to do with that fact that my mom and Demitrio used to date."

Oh, now *this* was interesting. "When?"

"Before Demitrio joined the army. After he left, my mom started seeing my dad."

"That had to be weird for your family. At least, I would think it would be. A torn-between-two-brothers situation."

"I suppose there could still be hard feelings. The truth is, I try to stay out of it."

It amazed her how he could be so clueless about what she considered blindingly obvious. That Demitrio could very well be Tony's father.

Is that why Tony's grandparents were so rough on Sarah when she and Tony Sr. first married? Did they know it was Demitrio's baby she was carrying? It sounded a little farfetched, but if she had learned one thing working as a bartender, it was that everyone had secrets, no matter their background or social status. It would be easy enough to figure out.

Meaning that if he really were Demitrio's son, *someone* would have figured it out by now.

She was letting her imagination get away from her. Again.

"Why the sudden interest in my uncle?" Tony asked, and she wondered if she should voice her suspicions, then decided it would probably be a bad idea. When things were going so well, why invite trouble?

"Just curious," she said, and he accepted the excuse without question. By the time they got to his apartment she had herself convinced she was being ridiculous. Mostly, anyway. Besides, it was none of her business.

Tony dropped her at the building and told her not to

wait while he found a parking spot, which at this time on a Friday night would probably be in Detroit.

When she heard him come in, she was already in her pajamas and sitting on the bed, digging around for her phone in her backpack.

Tony had tried to buy her a designer purse the other day, which she of course scoffed at. It astounded her that anyone in their right mind would pay hundreds of dollars for a leather shell with pockets, just for the name. She could eat for a month on that much money.

When the purse idea failed, Tony had suggested a new backpack—designer, of course—but she'd said no thanks to that, too. There was nothing wrong with the backpack she had, other than a few stains and worn spots, plus it had sentimental value. She picked it out of the lost and found at work the day Tony came into the bar for the first time.

"Wow, that was fast," Tony said, leaning in the bedroom doorway. "Already in your pajamas?"

"It's a wonder that I'm still conscious."

"Mind if I grab something from the closet?"

"Go for it," she said. Until they figured out a permanent living arrangement, they were sharing his closet. It was more than big enough for the both of them. Tony was a typical bachelor so the majority of his clothes never saw a hanger. They stayed in a basket beside the dryer until he dug them out and put them on. Thank goodness he owned a steam iron. And used it.

She looked at her phone and her heart stopped cold in her chest. "Oh, my God, he called."

Tony stepped out of the closet. "The doctor?"

"Ten minutes ago. My phone was in my backpack." Her heart started to pound so hard she felt light-headed.

"What kind of doctor calls a patient at nine on a Friday night?"

"A busy one."

"He left a message. I'm afraid to listen to it."

Tony walked over to her, hand out. "Give me the phone. I'll listen to it."

She dialed her voice mail and handed him the phone.

Tony listened for what couldn't have been more than ten seconds. "He left his cell number. Said to call when it was convenient. At any time."

Uh-oh. "How many doctors do that? And on a Friday night, no less."

He handed back her phone and sat down next to her, sliding his arm around her shoulder. "That doesn't mean it's bad news."

She put the phone on speaker then dialed the number.

Dr. Hannan answered after only two rings. "Good evening, Lucy."

"How did you know it was me?"

"Caller ID."

Of course. Duh.

"Everything is fine," he said.

"Huh?"

"You and the baby. You're both fine."

Oh, thank God. "You're absolutely sure?"

"Absolutely. The baby is small but healthy."

She was so relieved she could have sobbed. "Does this mean no more staying off my feet?"

"Well, I wouldn't go training for a marathon, but you can resume your normal activities. I'll see you in a month. If there's a problem before then, call the office."

"Okay. And thank you, Dr. Hannan."

"Good night Lucy."

She ended the call, looked up at Tony and promptly burst into tears.

Twice in one day? Really? What the heck was the matter with her?

Tony put his arms around her and she clung to him, soaking the front of his shirt with her tears, as he murmured reassurances, told her everything was going to be okay now. She desperately wanted it to be true. Yet she couldn't shake this impending sense of doom. Was this all just a little too good to be true? Was she going to wake up back at her mom's in Florida and realize it was all just a dream?

The outburst was blessedly short-lived, and when the tears finally stopped, Tony gave her a tissue and said, "Feel better?"

She sniffled and nodded. "Sorry. Guess I was a little stressed out."

He kissed her forehead, his stubble rough against her skin. "Everything is okay. You don't have to worry anymore."

This time, she wanted to say. So many things could still go wrong.

Tony cradled her face in his hands and looked into her eyes, which she was sure were watery and bloodshot. "Marry me," he said. "Don't even think about it. Just say yes."

The word balanced on the tip of her tongue. She wanted to so badly, but she couldn't. She didn't want a marriage of convenience.

"Lucy?"

There was something in his eyes this time, a look that, if she didn't know better, she might have mistaken for love.

Her mind was playing tricks on her again. She was

seeing what she wanted to see. "I know you think it's what's best for the baby—"

"Maybe it's what's best for me."

Well, obviously. Wasn't that why he kept asking her?

He realized what he said, shaking his head. "No. I didn't mean it like that. What I meant was, it would be best for *us*. All three of us."

She wasn't quite sure what he was trying to say. "But, technically, there is no *us*. Not beyond us being friends."

"Do you ever think that maybe there should be?"

More times than she could count. But not for the reason he was probably thinking. "I can't."

He blew out a frustrated breath. "You mean you won't."

Six of one, half a dozen of the other. "Can't...*won't*. What's the difference?"

"I can't accept that," he said.

He didn't have a choice.

"There has to be a way to convince you that this is the right thing to do. Just tell me what to say, what to do. What do you want?"

Tell me you love me and that you can't live without me, she wanted to say. Even if it wasn't true. She would probably say yes.

And if she did, she would be living a lie.

"You make me crazy," Tony said, pressing his forehead to hers. "If you could just..."

"Just what?" Compromise her principles? Her dignity?

He growled in frustration and pushed up off the bed, started pacing the floor like a caged animal. What had gotten his panties in such a twist?

"Look," she said. "I know you're probably used to getting what you want, but—"

He swiveled to face her. "Are you *kidding* me?"

She drew back at his sharp tone.

"When have I ever gotten what *I* want?"

She had no idea how to answer that, though she had the feeling it was a rhetorical question.

"I've stayed in a job, and a career, that I've grown to despise, because it's the right thing to do for the family." His tone grew more indignant with every word. "I have always done what I'm supposed to. And what has it gotten me? I can't even get the woman I love to marry me. So tell me again, how is it that I'm used to getting what I want?"

He'd lost her at *love*. She could hear him talking still, see his lips moving and hear the words, but the meaning wasn't getting through.

She cut him off midsentence. "What did you say?"

He opened his mouth to speak, then closed it again, his brow furrowing. "Which part?"

"When you said you love me."

He closed his eyes and cursed. "Sorry. I didn't mean to let that slip."

He was *sorry*?

"No," he said. "Screw that. I'm *not* sorry. I know it will probably only drive you farther away, but Lucy, I love you."

And *why* would that drive her away? She opened her mouth to respond but he kept going.

"I know that's probably the last thing you want to hear right now," he said.

The last thing? Really?

"For what it's worth, I did try to fight it. For your sake."

For *her* sake?

"And in the spirit of total honesty—"

"*Tony!*"

"What?"

"Shut up already," she said, and before he could say another word, she kissed him.

Nine

Lucy wasn't sure how she wound up on her back on the bed. Or how Tony managed to get their clothes off so fast. But damn, he sure did move quickly.

His scent, the flavor of his mouth, the rasp of his beard stubble against her skin were all so familiar, so Tony, yet this was as thrilling and exciting as the first time. She let her lids fall and felt the gentle sweep of his lips over hers.

"You are so beautiful," he said, gazing at her as if her skinny frame was a work of art. He trailed kisses across skin, kisses so steamy she could feel herself melting, sinking under. "Promise me you'll wear that dress again."

"What dress?" She ran her hands across his thick shoulders, urging him closer, but it was like trying to move a brick wall.

"The one you were wearing tonight," he said, running a hand up her thigh. "I like that it's soft and slippery...."

She gasped as he slipped his fingers inside of her and with a wicked smile said, "Just like you."

He stroked her, his touch unhurried and sweet one minute, and shockingly intimate the next, bringing her closer and closer to bliss. He kissed his way down, spreading her thighs apart, tasting her there, too. Sparks of desire popped and crackled, igniting her blood, and his breath on her skin worked like a soft breeze to fan the flames. He kissed and touched, murmuring sexy words that seemed to blend together and muddle up in her brain until they sounded like nonsense.

She threaded her fingers behind his neck, pulling him to her, his warm weight sinking her into the mattress. Every part of him felt warm and strong and solid. A shaft of moonlight from the bedroom window poured over him, accentuating every inch of his beautifully defined chest, his wide, solid shoulders and sinewy arms. He laced his fingers through hers, pinning her hands above her head. Then he rocked his hips just so, eased himself inside her with one long, slow, stroke....

Yes.

He gazed down at her, his eyes glassy and unfocussed, and said, *"Lucy."*

That alone nearly did her in. She was teetering on the edge of a cataclysmic explosion, the sparks snapping and sizzling, drawing ever closer to the end of her fuse.

He kissed her, a deep soul-searching kiss, while he tortured her with small thrusts of his hips. She clung to him, sinking her nails into his shoulders, his backside, her body arching with impatience. She'd never felt so out of control, so swept away with lust.

Tony muttered something unintelligible, then his grip on her hands tightened as every part of him began to tense. He thrust harder, taking Lucy to an entirely new level of ecstasy as the current pulled her under. Her own strangled moan was all she could hear, all she could comprehend, as the pleasure crashed down and dragged her under. Excruciating and perfect.

They were both breathing hard as Tony settled down beside her. She couldn't be one hundred percent positive, but she was pretty sure that pregnant sex was different from regular sex. It felt more...*passionate*. More intense.

Could that be what was causing her to feel even more confused, more unsure of herself, than ever?

This should be the happiest day in her life. Tony loved her and wanted to marry her and they were having a healthy baby. His family liked her and she liked them. She was getting everything she had ever wished for. She was supposed to feel happy. So, why did she still feel like a fraud?

Tony unwittingly gave her the answer. He curled up close, laying his head beside hers on the pillow. "I love you, Lucy."

He loved her? How could he, when he didn't even *know* her?

It seemed as though, when she fixed one disaster, another immediately cropped up in its place. When did it end? She must have made at least a few decent choices in her life. When did those start paying off? Or didn't it work that way?

She wanted him so much, wanted this. But not this way. Not knowing that at any moment something could come out about her past and he would never feel the same about her. He needed to know who and what she was. The good *and* the bad stuff. Luckily for her, this was an easy one to fix. All she had to do was tell him the truth. All of it. Then if he still wanted her, she would know she'd covered all her bases.

And after all this time of smothering the truth, of hiding it away, it would feel good to have it out there. To know that at least someone else out there knew.

"I wasn't completely honest with you about why I moved to Florida," she said.

He lay still beside her, listening.

Her heart started to beat faster and her hands were trembling. *Come on, Lucy, just say it.*

This truth thing was harder than she thought it would be. If she stopped for just ten seconds and let herself consider all the consequences…

Nope, bad idea. No more stalling or beating around the bush. She started this thing, now she was going to end it.

"Part of the reason I left, is because I was hoping you would come after me."

No reaction.

"Because…well…I guess because I fell in love with you and I was too afraid to tell you. I knew you were relationship-shy and, surprise, so am I. If you came after me, I would know you loved me. That's why I didn't tell you about the baby. I knew you would want to do the right thing, and it would have been too hard being married to a man who didn't love me."

She paused, expecting him to say something, then from beside her she heard a soft snore. Oh, no, he didn't…

She lifted up so she could see his face.

He was sound asleep.

Tony woke Saturday morning at ten-thirty, after the best night's sleep he'd had in a week.

Wow. Had it really only been a week? So much had happened since then. But last night had been a break-through in their relationship. Maybe the hard part was over now, and all they had to do was move forward. Start over in a sense.

He threw on his robe and went looking for Lucy, but all he found was a handwritten note placed on his laptop, which frankly scared the hell out of him. Maybe sleeping with her had been a bad idea. Had last night freaked her out so badly it sent her running back to Florida? He unfolded the note and started to read it.

Dear Tony,
I DID NOT leave you. Just thought I would get

*that out of the way, since that was probably the
first thing you thought of when you saw my note.*

He shook his head and smiled. She knew him too well.

*I'm with your mom. I called her this morning to let
her know that everything is okay with the baby and
she insisted we go shopping.*
*   You passed out on me last night, so I never got
to tell you how nice it was. Better than nice. I'm
really glad we're back to that place.*

Him, too. But…

Okay, so this is the part where I get serious.

Uh-oh.

*I love you. And I know that you think you love me,
but you can't really, because I'm not the woman
you think I am. That probably doesn't make much
sense, but it will. We have a lot to talk about. But
first I need you to do me a favor. Do you remember me telling you about my journal?*

Of course he did. It had been a school project that just
kept going. She would sometimes pull out her laptop and
write in it when she was hanging out at his place.

*I never thought I would hear myself say this to any-
one, but I want you to read it. I'll warn you that it's
very long and you're going to read a whole bunch
of stuff you wished you never knew. I'm sorry about*

*that. But you NEED to know. If after you read the
ENTIRE thing, you still want me (and I will totally
understand if you don't) my answer is yes, I would
love to marry you.*

    *I sent you an email link to the site and included
my user name and password.*
Love,
Lucy

Stunned, Tony set the letter down and for several minutes he just stood there, digesting it, looking at his closed
laptop, almost afraid to open it. She'd have to do something pretty awful to make him not love her. He was sure
that she was exaggerating....

But what if she wasn't?

Well, there was only one way to find out.

He fixed himself a strong cup of black coffee then
sat at the table and opened his computer. Her email was
waiting for him, with all the required information, so
with growing trepidation, he logged in, half hoping that
by some fluke it would deny him access. But up popped
her account.

It was sorted by year, going back to when she was
eleven years old. The most recent entry had been created
this morning at 5:40 a.m. He resisted the urge to skip to
the end and read the current stuff first, since it was probably the most relevant, and started at the very beginning.

The first few months had him yawning. It was the
usual preteen type stuff. What any girl would write in
her journal.

He couldn't escape the feeling that he was wasting his
time, and Lucy had some repressed, deep-seated flair for
the dramatic that was just now emerging.

Then the school project ended, and with it disappeared

that ideal, candy-coated world she had created. The first non-school post began, "Evicted again. Came home from school and all my stuff was in the Dumpster."

It went downhill from there.

After reading two more weeks' worth of entries, a knot began to grow in his gut. Two weeks more and he felt like vomiting. By the time he made it through the first year, he was seriously thinking of taking out a contract on Lucy's waste-of-a-life mom, who wasn't doing anyone any favors by being alive. He was Italian. He knew people who knew people.

He kept telling himself that it couldn't get any worse, but it always did. Thirteen-year-old girls wrote in their journal about the latest teen pop star or the boy they want to kiss. They did not write about their mom's *friend* copping a feel when her back was turned. Or waking in the middle of the night to find a different man snapping pictures of her while she was sleeping.

There were stupid people who didn't know any better, and bad people who knew and didn't care, then there were people like Lucy's mom, the kind who fed off other people's pain.

He'd taken a couple of psychology courses in college and he recognized the characteristics of a sociopath when he saw them. No one with a conscience would treat their child the way Lucy's mom had treated her.

Pure evil. That's what she was.

He thought of all the times he'd complained to Lucy about his family and felt utterly disgusted with himself. His childhood—his entire life—had been a freaking utopia compared to what she had been through.

She'd left home at seventeen and moved in with a friend. She'd been so full of hope that things could finally be better. But it wasn't long before the friend got a little too friendly one night, and when Lucy wasn't co-operative, she was out on the street. She seemed to drift through the next few years, moving around a lot, making new friends but never really connecting.

Heartbreaking. It was the only way to describe her life. Every time something good happened, five other things would blow up in her face. It seemed as though bad karma had taken a hold of her and wouldn't let go.

Then she'd met Tony.

Though it had been more than a year, the memory of that night, of seeing her behind the bar that first time, was scored in his memory.

Refreshing, that had been his first impression. She was young and vibrant and so pretty in her own natural way that he couldn't keep his eyes off of her. Apparently the feeling was mutual. A surprise to him considering they barely spoke the first half dozen times he came in. But according to her journal, it wasn't for a lack of interest. The way she told it, he was some sort of Greek god or something. She'd written one entire freaking page about his eyes. *Just* his eyes.

She'd done an amazing job of hiding it because he'd never had a clue. And when he'd asked her out, she'd told him she didn't date customers. The journal told a different story, that she thought he was too handsome and too nice, and therefore too good to be true. But gradually, over the next few weeks, he'd worn her down. That was the time when the tone of the journal really changed.

It was a bit like watching a flower unfold on time-lapse film. She'd gradually begun to open up, to trust him. To fall in love. She'd given him a gift. A window into her soul. And she was right. He would never look at her, or himself for that matter, the same way again.

Seeing himself through someone else's point of view

was intriguing and frightening, and brutally painful. But mostly just painful. A year of therapy couldn't compare to this slap-in-the-face, deal-with-it approach.

He considered it a miracle that after everything she had been through, all the hurt and the lies and the broken promises, she had opened up to him. She'd trusted *him*.

The responsibility of that knowledge was beyond overwhelming, and he was nearly 100 percent sure he hadn't deserved it, but he would never take trust for granted as long as he lived.

He heard a key in the lock, and looked up from the computer, his vision fuzzy from too much time reading the journal, to see the front door open. It was Lucy, her hair mussed from the wind. He was happy to see that his mother was not with her.

She stopped short when she saw him, looking surprised. "Are you sick?"

Did he look sick? "No, why?"

"It's six and you're still in your pajamas."

That meant he'd been sitting there riveted for almost seven hours. He hadn't eaten breakfast, or for that matter lunch. He hadn't even gotten up to use the bathroom. "I've been reading."

She blinked. "Oh…good."

Why did she not seem so sure of that? "That was a long shopping trip. Where's all the stuff?"

"Neither of us had the energy left to carry everything upstairs." She shrugged out of her jacket. "She said we can come by for dinner tomorrow and pick everything up. Except of course all the stuff that's being delivered."

Delivered?

"She bought furniture," Lucy said, looking pained. "I resisted, but there was nothing I could say to stop her."

She paused, chewing her lower lip, facing him, but not actually looking at him. "So, how much did you read?"

"Enough." Almost all of it.

"I have no idea where we'll put it. The furniture, I mean. You know, if we still…"

"What kind of furniture?"

"Baby furniture. It's maple, very gender neutral, and the crib turns into a toddler bed, which I assume is a good thing. It's a five-piece set."

"Well, I think that settles it, then," he said.

"Settles what?"

"Our living arrangements are going to have to change." He paused for dramatic effect, and he could see her holding her breath. "We need a bigger place."

"We as in you and the baby?"

"We as in all three of us."

"Like an apartment."

He shook his head. "Too impractical."

"Condo?"

"Nah. I think we need a house."

Ten

Lucy exhaled, then sucked in a lungful of air, feeling as if she hadn't actually taken a full breath since she left the apartment that morning. Then she took another, to try to stop the dizzy feeling in her head. "You want us to get a house? Together?"

"Isn't that what married people do? Have babies, buy houses. Live happily ever after. Stuff like that."

"You still want to marry me?"

"Isn't that what you do when you love someone?"

A giddy lightness settled over her. "I love you, too."

He pulled her into his arms and held her so tight. *Don't ever let go.* "I really thought that reading my journal would change the way you feel about me," she said, her voice muffled in his robe.

"It did change the way I feel. You were my best friend, my confidant, the woman I love." He tipped her face up so he could look in her eyes. "Now you're my hero."

She blinked. "Me? Someone's hero?"

"Lucy, you are by far the bravest person I've ever known."

"That's all well and good, but I'm still not the person you thought I was."

"No, you're not. You're better."

"Better?"

"Yes, better, and I couldn't love you more. Your past is what made you the person you are now, and *she* is the woman that I love."

"But…my background, my family…why would you want to be associated with that?"

"You are not your family, Lucy. And as far as I'm concerned, you never have to see that pathetic excuse for a mother ever again. In fact, I insist."

"She never wanted a baby," Lucy told him. "She was only interested in the child support check she could con out of some unsuspecting man. She hadn't counted on him dying so young."

"I'm surprised she didn't have more children to get more checks."

"She got an infection after I was born and they had to do a full hysterectomy. You could say that they shut down the baby factory before it could really get started."

"Divine intervention?"

"Could be." She laid a hand on her belly. "God forbid he takes after my side of the family."

"Lucy, if our child is anything like you, he'll be smart and strong and brave. He'll have real integrity, and a generous heart, and gifts that he will use to do beautiful, amazing things."

His words stole her breath. "Is that really how you see me?"

He touched her face. "When I grow up, I want to be just like you."

"Wow. I think that's the nicest thing anyone has ever said to me."

"It's about time someone said it. You have gifts, Lucy. Though I get the feeling you're not aware of a single one."

"I make a mean margarita."

"You listen to people. And I mean genuinely listen."

"I like hearing their stories. That's not really a gift."

"It is to the people telling the story. But you know what I realized after reading your journal? It's always someone else doing the talking. You have a voice, Lucy, and I know for a fact that you have an awful lot to say."

"What if I talked and no one listened?"

"Trust me, they'll listen."

"I'm not sure what it is you expect me to say."

"I'm going to suggest something that you're probably not going to like, but just hear me out, okay?"

"Okay."

"I think you should publish your journal."

Was he insane? "Publish, as in, make it available to the public? Do you have any idea how hard it was to show you? And you want everyone in cyberspace to read it."

"No, that's too limited. I think you should publish it in print."

She stepped back from him. He *had* to be joking.

"Hear me out, okay? What you went through…" He shook his head, as if he were refusing the images access to his mind. She knew just how he felt.

"You're not the only one. You could help people."

"How?"

"By showing them that they aren't alone. By using the voice that I know you have. Wasn't that the worst part for you? Feeling isolated and alone? Like no one could possibly understand? You can show people that there's hope."

She had never really considered that before.

"Despite it all, you made it, Lucy. You survived. Not everyone does."

She knew that better than anyone. "But…I'm not even a writer."

"Oh, yes you are."

"You really think so?"

"You have a gift, Lucy. Don't hide it away."

"Where would I even start?"

"I've got a friend from college, he's a literary agent. I'd like to send it to him, see what he thinks."

"I don't know, Tony."

"You could change people's lives. You've sure changed mine."

The idea of all those people reading about her life, especially Tony's family, terrified her. There were people who would identify, but also people who wouldn't. They would accuse her of exaggerating, or flat-out lying just for attention. Did she really want to open herself up to that kind of criticism? Or was it her obligation as a survivor, to help others in similar situations? Or for all she knew it could be a big flop and no one would buy it.

She didn't know what to do. "Let me think about it."

"Of course. I can call him Monday, see what he thinks. Oh, and by the way, please do not feel bad for Alice."

Wow, he really had gotten far in her journal. "I can't help it. I feel bad for her."

"It was a business arrangement, nothing more. No one walked away hurt. Not in the way you might be thinking."

"Even so, it had to be humiliating for her. Although it was nice of you to let her keep the ring."

"It was a small price to pay. That reminds me," Tony said. "I have something for you. Something I've been hanging on to for a long time. Just wait here. I'll go find it."

Exhausted from what had been, by far, the most eventful week of her entire life, Lucy collapsed on the sofa, kicked off her shoes and put her aching feet up on the coffee table.

Tony must not have been able to find what he was looking for because he came back a few minutes later empty-handed.

"Unlike you, I don't have a gift for words," he said. "It seems like half the time the things I say come out backward. So I want to be very clear about what I'm going to say. No frills, just the truth."

She was no expert, but she thought he was doing a pretty decent job already. Then he dropped to one knee in front of her and the air got stuck in her throat. *Hold on, Lucy. You're about to get everything you ever wanted in the whole world, but you are not, under any circumstances, going to cry again.*

"I love you, Lucy."

He was definitely off to a good start. "I love you, too."

From his robe pocket he pulled out a small, green velvet jewelry box that had yellowed a bit with age. He snapped it open and she actually gasped when she saw the ring inside. In the center sat a huge princess-cut diamond that shimmered in the sunlight pouring through the window. The diamond was surrounded by a ring of small rubies.

"Make my life complete, Lucy. Marry—"

"Yes!" she said. "Yes, yes, yes!"

He laughed again.

She smiled and said, "No frills. Just the truth."

"This was my great-grandmother's ring," he said, sliding it onto her finger.

"Your *nonna*'s mother?"

He nodded. "It's been in the family for over 100 years."

And he was entrusting it to her? She held up her hand. The diamonds glittered and the gold sparkled. She never imagined anything so lovely sitting on her finger. And it scared the hell out of her. What if she broke it, or God forbid, lost it?

"She died long before I was born," he said, "But being the oldest grandson, her ring was left to me."

"And you want *me* to wear it?" *Her,* not Alice.

"I put it on your finger, didn't I?"

Yes, and it was a perfect fit. His great-grandmother must have been a small person, like Lucy. It felt almost as if it was destined to be. Or maybe that was her imagination running away with her good sense again.

And if it was, so what? She was happy. Really, truly happy for the first time in her life. She felt as if anything was possible. And if she was going to dream, why not dream big?

They told his parents the good news at dinner the next night, and of course Tony's mom had to call his sisters. Precisely fifteen seconds later the entire family had heard the good news. Hell, maybe even the world. For almost two days after that the phone seemed to ring nonstop and the emails and cards began pouring in.

That would have annoyed him before, but Lucy's journal had forced him to reassess his priorities. He needed to stop being so judgmental and be happy that he had a family who loved and supported him unconditionally— even if they were big and loud and certifiably crazy. He was finished blaming them for his decision to stay with Caroselli Chocolate, because it was just that. *His* decision. He'd been either too lazy or too scared to leave the nest. Not anymore. Now there was no question that it would happen. It was just a matter of waiting for the right time.

First, though, it was important that he and Lucy and the baby were settled. That meant finding a house. But when he brought up the idea again she balked.

"You can't deny we need the space," he told her. Even with him back in his own bedroom, things would be tight. The baby would have to share an office with him. Or come to think of it, it was probably the other way around.

"Couldn't we just rent a bigger apartment?" she asked.

After she'd spent years living in flux, moving from one place to the next, never putting down roots, he would have thought she would jump at the chance to have a home of her own.

"A house would be a solid investment."

"And it would mean using the money that you've been saving to start your business."

Is that what this was about? Money? "Lucy, don't worry about where the money is coming from."

"Of course I'm going to worry! I know it was rough after the recession. And I also know you've been trying to save money. I'm not going to let you blow it all on a house we don't need."

Clearly she had been making assumptions.

Wildly inaccurate ones.

"Lucy, do you have any idea what I make a year?"

She shook head and said, "Not a clue. But you drive a BMW, so I assumed you do pretty well."

He'd been living so far beneath his means to save money, it was no wonder she was confused. And he had the feeling she was in for the shock of her life.

He told her his salary, and his estimated net worth. Though he had to admit, the look on her face was worth at least double that.

"Did you say, *million?*" she asked, her eyes like saucers. "As in, you're a *millionaire?*"

"I thought you knew."

"You did say million, right?"

"I did. So, now can we buy a house?"

"Yeah, sure," she said, looking a little dazed. "Let's buy a house."

He called his real estate guy that afternoon, told him to start looking immediately. Within two days he had a long list of houses lined up to see over the weekend. Most were newish, with all the good upgrades.

Saturday wound up being a bust. Tony liked several of the homes, but Lucy kept insisting that they were either too big or too expensive—or both. And he couldn't deny that most of them didn't have nearly the yard space they were hoping for.

Sunday was shaping up to be another epic fail, until their agent got a call from his assistant about a house that had just been placed on the market.

"It's a fixer-upper," he told them. "In an up-and-coming neighborhood. If you're looking for a good investment, this is it. They're asking under market value, so I'm guessing it will go fast."

"Can't hurt to look." That would give them a couple of months to make it habitable before the baby was born.

The house was an old Victorian with five bedrooms and a huge wraparound porch, and unlike the newer, cookie-cutter homes they had seen so far. The street was slightly run-down, but reasonably safe, and yes, up-and-coming. But the structure itself looked as if a strong breeze were all it would take to knock it over.

"It's perfect," Lucy said.

Perfect? Was she was nuts? "It's falling apart."

"But it could be so beautiful."

"Well, let's look." He could only imagine what horrors lay ahead for them inside. But honestly, it wasn't as bad as he expected. Every room needed renovations, but the foundation looked sound. The cost wasn't an issue, but the amount of time it might take to complete them could be.

"I love it," she said when they stepped outside with the Realtor. "It's everything I could ever want in a house. It has the space we need, and look how huge the yard is. It just needs a little TLC."

It needed way more than that, but the excitement in her eyes, the flush of her cheeks, said she had made up her mind. And if this was really what she wanted, she would have it. "It could take months to finish the renovations," he told her.

"Meaning the three of us will have to live in the apartment until it's done. It's going to be cramped"

"That's a sacrifice I'm willing to make."

"So have we made a decision?" the real estate agent asked.

Lucy looked up at Tony hopefully, her eyes pleading with him. He turned to the Realtor and said, "If this is the house she wants, this is the house we'll get."

Lucy threw her arms around Tony and squeezed hard. "Thank you!"

The agent looked pretty pleased as well. "Great! Why don't we go back to my office and draw up the offer."

They put in a cash offer for ten percent over the asking price. Within an hour it was accepted by the owner, and the following Tuesday, the contractor started the renovations.

On the one month anniversary of Lucy being back, Tony surprised her with a brand-new, top of the line minivan with all the bells and whistles. Built-in car seats, a premium sound system with a DVD player and navigation system. And more importantly, a stellar safety rating.

With wedding plans also underway, things were a lit-

tle hectic, but Tony felt as if everything was falling perfectly into place.

He should have realized that was only the calm before the storm.

Eleven

The week after Easter, which was a crazy-hectic holiday for a chocolate maker, Tony was finally enjoying a quiet day at work, when Rob burst into his office, wired and short of breath.

"Grab your jacket. We have to go."

"Where?"

"No time to explain. Nick is meeting us in the garage."

Tony grabbed his jacket and followed Rob, who was sprinting toward the elevator.

"Could you at least tell me where we're going?" Tony asked as they rode down to the parking garage.

"*Nonno*'s house."

Tony's knees nearly buckled. "What happened? Is he okay?"

"He's fine. Everyone is fine."

He wasn't acting that way, and what did he mean by *everyone*?

Nick was in his car waiting for them. Rob hopped in the front and Tony got in back—which was not exactly a comfortable place to sit for a guy over six feet tall.

"Could someone please tell me what's going on?" Tony said as Nick peeled out onto the street.

Rob turned in his seat. "It would seem we were right about Rose."

Oh, hell. "What did she do?"

"She showed up at *Nonno*'s this morning, asking to see him. Claimed to be a friend of the family."

"William didn't let her in, did he?"

"William didn't answer the door. And now that she's there, she won't leave. She wants an audience with *Nonno*."

"Why?"

"Good question."

"I'm confused," Tony said. "If William didn't let her in, who did?"

Looking pained, Rob glanced over to Nick, who nodded. "Dude, it was Lucy."

His seven-and-a-half-months pregnant fiancée was stuck in *Nonno*'s house with a crazy person? Lucy had never met Rose, so she wouldn't have known not to let her in. "I thought you were supposed to be looking into this," he told Rob.

"I looked. There was nothing to find. She is who she says she is. She just happens to be nuts, too."

Fantastic.

The drive to *Nonno*'s never felt so long. His uncle Demitrio's car was already there, parked behind a late model sedan in the driveway. He half expected to see police cars with their lights flashing. Wouldn't someone have called the police by now?

Tony was the first one out of the car, and the first to bust through the door into the foyer where William met him. "Where are they?"

"The great room," William said.

His dad and both his uncles stood by the bar, talking quietly amongst themselves.

And sitting on the couch, *holding Rose's hand,* was Lucy.

Huh?

When she saw Tony, Lucy smiled. A smile that said, *It's okay, stay calm, everything is under control.* She whispered something to Rose, who nodded and let go of Lucy's hand. Lucy stood, gesturing for Tony and his cousins to follow her. She led them out of earshot, to the hallway outside the kitchen.

"What the hell is going on?" Tony asked. "Why hasn't someone called the police?"

"Because other than being stubborn about talking to *Nonno,* she really hasn't done anything wrong," Lucy said. "I don't believe that she's dangerous, or wants to physically hurt anyone."

"Lucy, this kind of behavior is not normal."

"Oh, I never said she's normal. The cheese definitely slid off her cracker, but she doesn't seem violent."

"Why is she here?" Nick asked.

"Well, the gist of it is, she believes that she's *Nonno*'s illegitimate daughter."

"That's ridiculous," Rob said.

Tony would have to agree. She didn't look a thing like any of the Carosellis. She may have had similar coloring, but that was where any resemblance ended. Besides, it would have meant that *Nonno* had an affair with his secretary, and he would never do something like that. He loved their *Nonna,* practically kissed the ground she walked on. He would never cheat on her.

"She tells a very convincing story," Lucy said. "For a crazy person, I mean. Personally, I think she's just a very lonely, confused individual who needs professional help."

"Why didn't William answer the door?" Nick asked.

"He was upstairs helping *Nonno* into bed. I opened the door and she just sort of marched in like she belonged here. She told me that she was family, but she seemed kind of nervous and twitchy, like she was waiting for a SWAT team to crash through the window. It took a few minutes but I finally got her to tell me her name. I excused myself to the bathroom and called Sarah. She called your dad. He and his brothers have been trying to talk to her since they got here, but she only wants to talk to *Nonno.*"

"Then talk to me she shall."

Everyone turned to see *Nonno* shuffling toward them, William at his side. *Nonno* looked so old and frail. So vulnerable.

"Are you sure that's a good idea?" Rob asked. "She's clearly not stable."

Instead of relying on one of his grandsons to help him, he gestured to Lucy. "Take me to her."

Without question Lucy slipped an arm through his to lead him there. When had they become such close pals?

"I'm still not convinced this is a good idea," Rob said.

Neither was Tony, but he trusted Lucy's judgment. More than a few times he had seen her deal with unruly bar patrons. She had a way with people.

When Rose saw *Nonno,* she sprang to her feet and demanded, "Tell them the truth."

"And what truth would that be, young lady?" *Nonno* asked, wincing as Lucy helped him into a chair close to the couch. Too close, as far as Tony was concerned. He stepped up beside Lucy, laying a hand on her shoulder. Just in case.

"That I'm your daughter," Rose said, her voice trembling, her movements jittery.

Nonno's sons all moved a few steps closer.

"I assure you that you are not," *Nonno* told her.

"I found the letters after she died. I know what you did." She turned to his sons. "I know all about this family and their secrets."

What the hell was that supposed to mean? Tony started to take a step forward but Lucy grabbed his arm.

"Do you deny writing love letters to my mother? Do you deny having an affair with her?"

Looking totally unfazed by the accusation, *Nonno* said, "I deny nothing. But that doesn't mean you're my daughter."

Did he really just admit to having an *affair?*

Tony waited for a collective gasp from everyone in the room, but he, his cousins and Lucy were the only ones who looked surprised. Could their parents have known about this all along?

"I want a paternity test," Rose said.

"That won't be necessary." *Nonno* leaned forward in his chair. "If you knew so much about my family, young woman, I wouldn't have to tell you that I had a vasectomy almost fifty years ago. How old are you Rose?"

Rose blinked several times, clearly confused. "No," she said, shaking her head. "That can't be right. You're lying."

She looked more devastated than dangerous, but Demitrio had apparently had enough, and stepped between them. "I know for a fact that he's not lying, and it will be easy enough to prove with medical records. Which you will be able to obtain through our lawyer. Until then I have to insist that you stay away from my family. And that includes my daughter Megan. I'll see that your things are packed and sent wherever you desire."

Rose's chin tipped up a fraction, and she smiled vaguely, looking slightly maniacal, as if someone had flipped a switch in her brain, and let the crazy out. "You're very confident, Demitrio, for someone with so much to hide." Her voice eerily calm, she turned to Rob, Tony and Nick. "Wouldn't you agree, boys?"

Demitrio didn't even flinch. "William, will you show our guest out please? And if she comes back, call the authorities."

Tony pulled his cell phone out, ready to dial 911 if she refused to leave again. But this time she went without argument.

For several minutes everyone just stood there in uncomfortable silence. There was something up. Tony could feel it.

"Wow," Nick finally said. "She must have had an extra helping of crazy with her breakfast."

"What did she mean when she said she knows the family's secrets?" Tony asked his dad. "What secrets?"

Everyone exchanged looks, but no one spoke, and he had the uncomfortable feeling that everyone knew what was going on except him. That theory solidified when he realized that no one would look him in the eye.

"Isn't anyone else curious?" he asked the room in general.

"She's a loon," Nick said. "I don't think she even knew what she was saying."

"It's over," *Nonno* said, ruling out further discussion. "I'm tired. I need to rest."

He gestured to Lucy instead of William to help him, and she took his arm.

Tony could have stopped him, insisted that someone tell him what the hell was going on. He didn't. He wasn't sure if he really wanted to know.

"Am I correct in assuming you three already knew about *Nonno*'s affair?" Tony said, turning to his dad and uncles.

His dad nodded. "We knew. But it's not the sort of thing you bring up at family dinner. He was not a perfect man. None of us are."

He looked at Tony when he said it, but Tony had a feeling those words were meant for someone else. Not that he considered himself perfect. Far from it. But when it came to secrets, his life was pretty much an open book. He'd done nothing he felt the need to hide.

Well, almost nothing.

"Everyone should go," Demitrio said. "Let *Nonno* rest."

He and Lucy were the last to leave, and when he finally had her alone, he pulled her into his arms and held her. "When Rob told me you were trapped here with Rose, I expected the worst. The idea that you might have been hurt..." He squeezed her tighter. "I don't know what I would have done."

She pushed up on her toes and kissed him. "I'm tougher than I look."

And braver than even he realized.

Lucy gave Tony a ride back to the office to get his car, and since she had never seen it, and it was still business hours. Tony took her on a tour of the building. Nick even gave his permission to visit the top floor, the kitchen where he oversaw the creation of all new products. An honor bestowed upon a scarce few.

He saved his office for last.

He introduced her to his secretary. Though they had never met in person, Lucy had talked on the phone with Faedra numerous times in the past couple of weeks and they greeted one another like old friends. By the time he managed to drag Lucy away they were planning to meet for lunch so Faedra could give her a box of baby stuff. As if she couldn't give the stuff to Tony, who could then take it home. More likely they were just looking for an excuse to get together and eat. Tony never understood why an excuse was even necessary. If he wanted to go to lunch, he went to lunch. Being hungry was reason enough.

It was definitely a chick thing.

"Wow, it's big," she said, when they stepped into his office, then turned to him and grinned. "Not the first time I've said that to you, huh?"

Oh, no, she was getting that look in her eyes, the one that said he should probably lock the door. He and Lucy had always had a very enthusiastic sex life. But lately she had been insatiable. Some days she would chase him down two, and sometimes three times, not that he was complaining. She was already at the window closing the blinds, and though they had made love that morning, she was obviously ready for more.

He locked the door and tugged his tie loose, watching as Lucy pulled her dress over her head and dropped it to the floor. Her bra went next, and damn…he could swear that she looked sexier and more beautiful every time he laid eyes on her.

He unbuttoned his shirt, and was about to take it off when she stopped him.

"Keep it on," she said, unfastening his pants, sliding a hand inside. She kissed him, nibbling his lip. She knew just what to do to make him crazy. "It's sexy when I'm naked and you're dressed. It feels like we're doing something naughty."

There was one particular part of him that seemed to think so, too; it pulsed in her hand. But her expanding belly and his height were forcing them to get creative with positions. "Where to? In the chair, on the desk?"

With a hungry grin she slid her panties down, turned away from him and leaned across the surface of his desk, looking back at him over her shoulder. "Come and get it."

With a sigh of satisfaction, Lucy stretched out beside Tony in bed. From the looks of it, the way he was draped across the mattress half-conscious, she had worn him out again. He was so whipped he'd texted his secretary and told her he would be in late, and to reschedule any meetings.

"I don't know why you're so tired," she said. "I did all the work that time."

And her thighs would pay the price tomorrow.

"I'm tired," he said. "Because I'm old."

"What are you? Thirty-eight? Thirty-nine? That's not very old."

He glared at her. "You know I'm thirty-five."

She grinned back. "Thirty-five isn't old. I don't even consider your parents to be *old* old. Old is *Nonno*'s age."

"What's with you and him, by the way? You're like buds now."

Lucy smiled. "I like being around him. I love to listen to his stories. He's had such an interesting life."

"If that isn't the understatement of the century."

"It was kind of a shock about the affair. When I was helping him to his room he asked if I was disappointed in him."

"Are you?"

"Without knowing the circumstances? Who am I to judge? There are a million reasons why it could have happened." She pushed up on her elbow. "Are you?"

"I'm not sure what to think. I'd like to feel outraged on *Nonna*'s behalf, but you're right, I don't know the circumstances. Maybe she knew and didn't care."

"Or participated," Lucy said.

"Please," he said, looking pained. "Let's not go there."

The baby started to kick so she took Tony's hand and laid it on her belly. She swore she could actually feel the baby growing. In the past month, her stomach had swelled to what seemed like gigantic proportions on her small frame. At her appointment yesterday the doctor estimated that the baby had grown a third in size since her first visit.

Tony was quiet for several minutes, but she could feel him building up to something, and she was pretty sure she knew what.

"Today, at *Nonno*'s, I got the impression that they all knew something I didn't," he said. "Would you know anything about that?"

She thought the same thing, and of course, she had a theory....

Oh, no you don't. She had no right to go stirring up trouble for him. Of course, it was *just* a theory, and anything she told him would be pure speculation.

"Lucy?"

She was probably going to regret this. "I do have an idea."

"Let me have it," he said. "What am I missing?"

She sat up, suddenly feeling edgy and unsettled. Maybe this wasn't such a great idea. "This is pure speculation, and I'm sure has no basis in reality."

He pushed himself up on his elbows, the sheet draped across his thighs, the shadow of a beard darkening his cheeks. It could very well have been the sexiest thing she'd ever seen.

"Okay," he said, "go ahead."

"I think..." She paused, giving herself one last chance to reconsider.

"Yes?"

"I think maybe Demitrio is your father."

Mumbling a curse, he collapsed onto his back. "I was afraid you were going to say that."

"So I'm not telling you anything you didn't already suspect?"

"Knowing my mom dated Demitrio, how could I not? I guess I just never let myself think about it."

"It would explain a lot of things, like why your grandparents were so rough on your mom. And why you look so much like Demitrio."

"I want to know, and at the same time I don't."

"Knowing who my real father was never benefited me. Of course, mine was an adulterer who knocked up a seventeen-year-old."

"Maybe it's time I have a talk with my mom."

His phone started to ring, and Lucy half expected it to be Sarah. Tony checked the display. "It's Richard Stark."

Lucy's heart skipped a beat. Though it had taken an awful lot of convincing, she had let Tony send her journal to his agent friend. She figured the odds of him actually wanting to represent it were slim to none. He was probably calling to tell them, in so many words, that it sucked.

And what if he isn't? What if he actually loved it?

"You want to talk to him?" Tony asked.

She wouldn't have the first clue what to say. "Can you see what he wants?"

He answered the phone. And after a few minutes of random chitchat, Tony's expression turned serious. For the next minute or two he did a lot of nodding, and said things like "I see" and "If you think that's best." And it was obvious, by his grim expression, that the news wasn't good.

Oh, well, it had been a long shot at best. It was a relief to know that the entire world wouldn't be privy to her private thoughts, yet a small part of her was just a tiny bit disappointed.

They talked for a minute more, then Tony hung up.

"So," he said, setting his phone back on the table. "Richard read your journal."

"And he thought it stank," she said, holding her breath, waiting for the inevitable rejection.

"He loved it."

Wait, what? "He does not."

"Yes, he does."

No way. She'd barely graduated high school. Writers were college educated and far more worldly than she could ever be. Weren't they? "You're screwing with me."

"He said it was poignant and heartbreaking."

"No way."

"He'd like to represent you. He stressed that it was going to be a hard sell, and said not to get your hopes up. He said to think it over and give him a call."

"Oh my gosh," she said, feeling as if she were the victim of some elaborate joke. Or sound asleep and dreaming. "This is unbelievable."

"And I'm not the least bit surprised," he said. "I'm convinced someone will buy it."

After so many years of being told by her mom that she would never amount to anything, Lucy had begun to believe her. But here she was, one step closer to possibly being a real published author. She was dizzy with excitement.

"So, will you accept his representation?"

If it meant possibly helping people, how could she not at least try? Proving her mom wrong, that was just the icing on the cake.

"I honestly never imagined something like this could happen to me," she told Tony.

"Whether or not you believe it, you're an extraordinary woman, Lucy."

"Thank you so much," she said, throwing her arms around him.

"I did nothing. This was all you."

He couldn't be more wrong.

She held his face in her hands. "No. Without you, I never would have had the courage to give it to an agent in the first place. You have faith in me, and that gives me faith in myself."

"From the second I met you, I knew that you were destined for great things," he said.

It was a little weird, but she was actually starting to believe him.

Twelve

For days Tony debated with himself about what to do. Should he talk to his mom? His dad? Uncle Demitrio? If they had lied to him for this long, what made him think they would tell him the truth now?

His subconscious must have decided for him. After a lunch meeting he left the restaurant and headed back to work. The next thing he knew, he was pulling into his parents' driveway.

He made a quick call, then walked to the porch. His mom opened the front door before he even had a chance to knock.

"What a nice surprise!" she said, flashing him a mega-watt smile. One that didn't quite reach her eyes. "Come in, I just brewed a pot of coffee."

He followed her into the kitchen. "I'm not thirsty."

She didn't seem to hear him. "I'll pour you a cup."

She scurried from cupboard to cupboard, pulling out cups, then the sugar and milk, even though they both drank their coffee black.

Lucy was like that, never staying in one place for long.

Always up and moving, getting things done. Living life with an almost childlike fascination for the world around her. Always finding a silver lining no matter how dark and ominous the overhead clouds were.

Come to think of it, his mom and Lucy were an awful lot alike.

She set a cup of coffee that he wouldn't drink on the counter beside him, along with the milk and sugar he wouldn't use. It was amusing in a way, to see her so nervous, since it was such a rare occurrence. But it didn't bode well for him.

"I suppose Dad told you about the incident at *Nonno*'s. How Rose said she knows our secrets."

"I knew from the start that there was something wrong with that woman." She busied herself filling her cup. "I told your father she's unstable."

"Funny you should mention my father," he said.

They both knew something was up, so why not get to the point? He was a man of few words and this small talk thing they were doing was getting annoying fast.

"Mom, I think you know why I'm here. Why don't you just say whatever it is you have to say? After all these years, think of what a relief it would be to finally tell me."

She lifted a trembling hand to cover her mouth, tears brimming in her eyes.

"Is Demitrio my father?"

She squeezed her eyes shut, as if she couldn't bear to see the look on his face when she nodded and she said, "Yes, he is."

And here Tony thought he was prepared for this. Was he ever wrong. Thinking it might be true and actually knowing it were two completely different animals. Had it not been for reading Lucy's journal, he would probably have stormed out by now. The hell she went through really put things in perspective.

Even if the man who had raised him wasn't his biological father, Tony had never wanted for a thing growing up. He'd been raised by two parents who loved and took care of him. Wasn't that what mattered?

He heard the front door open and his heart skipped a beat. When his dad and Uncle Demitrio stepped into the room, what little color remained in his mom's face leached away. Her voice trembling, she asked, "What are you two doing here?"

"I asked them to come," Tony said. And it was clear, by the stoic look both men wore, that the jig was up. "We're going to talk about this. We should have talked about it a long time ago."

Demitrio and his mom glanced at each other, then quickly looked away. His dad stared at the floor, shaking his head.

Their unwillingness to cooperate set his nerves on edge. "You owe me the truth. Act like the adults you're supposed to be and talk to each other. Talk to me."

Demitrio frowned. "Watch your tone."

He had a lot of nerve issuing orders. Tony strapped down his anger, looked him in the eyes and said, "You don't get to tell me what to do."

"I am your father," he said.

No, Tony realized. He wasn't. The man who raised him was his real father. Antonio Caroselli Senior. Even if he was absent for the conception. And that would never change.

"I love you, and I think you're a great guy, but you are *not* my father. That's an earned title."

Demitrio winced. "I didn't expect that to sting so much."

He should have considered that thirty-five years ago.

"I had always hoped that one day we could have a father-son relationship," Demitrio said.

"Maybe, if you hadn't waited until now to admit the truth, we could have."

That stung too. Tony could tell.

"We did what we thought was best for you," his dad said. "It was a complicated situation."

"Did you know my mom was pregnant when you left?" Tony asked Demitrio.

"Not when I left. But when I heard she was pregnant later, I suspected that you could be mine. But your mom was already married to my brother, so what could I do? I didn't find out the truth until you were nearly a teenager."

"If you suspected, you could have asked."

"But I didn't. And I will regret that for the rest of my life."

"Is that supposed to make me feel better?"

His dad stepped up to his brother's side. "If you need to blame someone for this," his dad said, "blame me. I'm the one who convinced your mom not to tell him. And when the truth did finally come out, I was the one who made Demitrio swear not to tell you. He wanted you to know. And lately he's been pressuring us to tell you. We weren't ready."

"Were you ever going to be ready?"

"You have to understand the position we were in," his mom said. "We only wanted what was best for you."

"Lying to me?" Tony asked, anger and resentment dripping from every word. He was trying to keep an open mind, see things from their side, but all he was hearing were hollow excuses. "I've yet to hear a single excuse that would indicate you had even a modicum of regard for my feelings. In fact, it sounds a lot like you were just covering your own asses."

"Were we selfish?" Demitrio said. "Absolutely. Anyone with eyes could see the way you struggled as a teenager. Always there, but slightly in the background. Listening, but not really participating. It was like watching myself. I knew that you needed the stability of a cohesive family. It's what I believed was best for you. When you were born I was thoughtless, aimless and immature, and until I got my act together I wouldn't have been any kind of father to you. It would have only complicated your life."

"And later, when I was an adult?"

"Sweetheart," his mom said, "you're a grown man about to become a father. Try putting yourself in our position. Suppose for whatever reason you and Lucy hadn't reconnected, and fourteen years later you found out you had a child. What would your answer be when she demands to know why you've never been there?"

That was a good question. And who was he to judge them? He'd been so totally oblivious that he nearly lost out on the opportunity to know his own child.

When Lucy left, he knew deep down that something was wrong, and he knew he should go after her. If only to be sure that she was all right. He'd been too much of a coward. There was that voice in his head saying she was with someone else. Someone better. So of course the logical solution was to find someone else too. A kind of *so there*.

What a horrible mistake that had turned out to be. His parents weren't perfect. But he did know they loved him, and he had to trust them. He had to give himself time to be angry and resentful, then accept the past and get over it.

"Is this why the two of you have been at each other's throats?" Tony asked.

Demitrio nodded. "I've been pushing your parents to tell you."

"But I knew something was going on with you," his mom said. "Call it a mother's intuition. I wasn't sure what it was, but there was something.

That must have been right around the time that Lucy left, the most retched couple of months of his life. What would have happened had they, on top of that, tossed in an uncle who was really a biological father. He shuddered to think.

"It was wrong the way I acted," Demitrio told them, head hung in contrition. "I overstepped my bounds. I was presumptuous and arrogant in my belief that I knew what was better for him. Clearly I did not."

"None of this would be happening if it wasn't for me," his mom said, her eyes tearing up. "I should have told you the truth from the start. I'm so sorry, Demitrio."

This was shifting in a direction Tony would rather not travel. "It sounds as if you three need some time to talk," he told them.

"Will you ever forgive us?" his mom asked, looking so distraught he had to smile.

"Of course," he said, putting his arms around her and squeezing hard. His dad put his arms around the both of them. Standing a few feet away, Demitrio looked outcast and alone, and a tightness in Tony's chest eased.

"Bring it in," he told Demitrio, gesturing him over. Demitrio hesitated, then moved in closer, wrapping his arms around all three of them.

He was going to follow Lucy's lead this time and focus on what was most important. The other stuff could wait.

Right now, he just wanted to go home and hug the woman of his dreams. The mother of his baby.

The love of his life.

Thirteen

Lucy and Tony's wedding day turned out to be the most magical day of her life.

She'd never been to a formal wedding, nor had she ever expected to get married, so she was totally clueless when it came to the task of planning one. But Sarah and Tony's sisters Chris and Elana, and Nick's sister Jessica, were more than happy to do it all for her. And they spared no expense.

With the help of a wedding planner, they transformed the backyard of his parent's mansion, which sat on the shore of Lake Michigan, into a vision of satin swags, delicate pink roses, and twinkling, miniature white lights. As Tony's parents walked with her down the aisle, one on either side, she felt a little like Cinderella on her way to the ball. And with her due date only a week away, a hugely pregnant one.

When Lucy saw Tony waiting for her at the steps of the gazebo dressed in a tuxedo, looking more handsome than she'd ever seen him, her heart felt like it would burst with happiness.

They spoke their vows at sunset, the waves of Lake

Michigan crashing against the shore behind them. As they exchanged rings, and kissed for the first time as man and wife, Lucy knew without a doubt that she had found her happily ever after.

After the ceremony, Tony's parents threw them a reception in their backyard. First came a delicious, four-course meal, then the cutting of the cake, then she and Tony were called onto the dance floor for their first official dance. After that, in true Caroselli form, the reception turned into a bash. The alcohol flowed, and a DJ blasted dance music over enormous speakers. When the neighbors enquired about the noise, they were invited to join in. By the time Lucy helped *Nonno* to the spare bedroom to rest later that evening, she was pretty sure half the neighborhood was there.

It was the perfect wedding. The perfect day.

Right up until the second that it wasn't anymore.

Lucy was on her way back outside when she ran into Carrie, Rob's wife, just outside the bedroom. She was blonde and pretty and nearly as petite as Lucy, with a cute little baby bump under a formfitting top.

Other than the occasional, obligatory greeting at family functions, she and Lucy avoided each other. They never spoke of it, but it was obvious that Carrie held Lucy responsible for what happened to Alice.

"Nice wedding," Carrie told her, and though she sounded sincere, there was something in her eyes, the way she was looking at Lucy, that set Lucy's nerves on edge.

"Much nicer than his *last* wedding," Carrie added.

This was ridiculous. Like it or not they were family now. Couldn't they find a way to bury the hatchet?

"Carrie, I know you don't like me, and I don't blame you for feeling that way."

"That's charitable of you," Carrie said, not even trying to hide her disapproval.

"For what it's worth, I'm really sorry about what happened to Alice."

"Getting dumped at the altar, you mean? Call me crazy, but you sure didn't look sorry. Alice on the other hand was devastated."

Twist the knife a little deeper. Oh, yeah, this was not shaping up to be a pleasant conversation. Maybe tonight was the wrong time to bring this up. Maybe the sad truth was that she and Carrie would never get past this.

"I should get back outside," Lucy said, hoping that would be the end of it. But when she tried to leave, Carrie stepped in her way.

"Do you know what you're having?" she asked, but there was something dark and calculating in her expression. What was she up to?

"I wanted it to be a surprise, but I'm pretty sure it's a boy. I feel like it is."

"I'll bet Tony is pretty happy about that."

"Sure." What man wouldn't be excited about having a son? Though she was sure he would be just as happy with a daughter.

"So how does it feel to be walking around with thirty million dollars in your belly?"

Lucy frowned, getting a very bad feeling. "I have no idea what you're talking about."

"Tony's deal with his grandfather. He'll get thirty million for producing a male heir. That's the only reason he was going to marry Alice. They had a deal. But then along you came, already pregnant. Rather convenient, don't you think?"

It wasn't true. She was just messing with Lucy, playing with her emotions. "If you say so."

"But first he had to marry you. That was part of the deal. And now he has."

It was a lie. She knew it was. Carrie's way of getting back at her for hurting Alice. It *couldn't* be true.

"Ask him. He'll tell you."

Carrie would love that, wouldn't she? If she made such a horrible accusation Tony would be hurt that she didn't trust him.

This time when Lucy tried to walk away, Carrie let her pass, calling after her, "Enjoy the rest of your party."

She would, damn it. She would not let this ruin the happiest day in her life.

Brushing off the bad vibes, Lucy walked through the family room to the French doors that led out onto the deck. But when she put her hand on the knob, she couldn't seem to make it turn.

Tony loves you, he's your husband, you have to trust him. Go to him, have fun.

But her feet betrayed her. She walked back to the spare room instead. Heart in her throat, she knocked softly, half hoping *Nonno* was asleep.

"Yes," he called.

She opened the door and found him sitting on the edge of the bed, almost as if he'd been waiting for her. He would tell her that it was a terrible lie.

"I need to talk to you."

He looked so tired and sad. "I know."

"Did you hear what Carrie said to me?"

He nodded.

"Is it true?"

"Why don't you ask your husband?"

Oh, no. No, no, no. "Because I'm asking you. Did you offer Tony money to have a male heir?"

"The Caroselli name was about to die out, and those boys aren't getting any younger. They needed incentive."

Her heart splintered, then split down the middle, with a pain so intense she couldn't draw a full breath. "You were supposed to be my friend. The grandfather I never had. How could you plot behind my back like that? How could you not tell me?"

Pride leveled his chin. "My loyalty will always be to my grandson. Family comes first."

"I don't have a family. I thought I did. Clearly I was mistaken." She turned, started to walk out.

"Lucy, stop." He wasn't used to people walking away from him, and when she didn't stop immediately, his tone went from arrogant and entitled to pleading. "Lucy. Please. This was my fault."

She paused just outside the door, despair tugging at her soul.

"Don't make Tony pay for my mistake. He's a good man. A loyal grandson."

She turned to him. "But not a very loyal husband."

At least now she knew why Tony was so eager to marry her, and why he waited until *after* the ultrasound to propose a second time. All those things he said about her being his hero…were those lies, too? Just a way to manipulate her? Was anything he said to her true?

"Lucy, he loves you."

He had an unusual way of showing it. "I'm sure you'll understand when I say that sometimes that's just not enough."

She closed the door and walked away, not even sure where she was going, reminding herself to breathe. Inhale, exhale. Breathe in, breathe out. Every part of her ached. Even her hair seemed to throb. Old wounds in her heart swelled, then burst, poisoning her blood with the vile seeds of hurt and rejection. She felt like she was falling apart, one piece at a time.

The repercussions were almost too much to bear. This was why Tony was okay about buying a house, and spending so much of his money. He *knew* he had a big chunk of money coming in when the baby was born. He knew he was set.

Congratulations, Mom, you hit the nail on the head. Men like him only kept girls like her around for one reason. And she sure had been keeping him happy in that department lately, hadn't she? He'd played her, and the worst part was that she didn't know if he even realized he was doing it.

"Lucy?"

She turned to see Tony standing behind her and her knees went weak. He was so beautiful it hurt to look at him. How could he do this to her?

Looking worried, he said, "Is everything okay?"

Talk about a loaded question. She refused to give Carrie the satisfaction of knowing she had ruined Lucy's wedding, even if it was all just an illusion. A deal between relatives.

Because family always came first.

She pasted on a smile and said, "I'm just tired, and I've had a nagging backache all afternoon."

At least that much was true.

"I'm exhausted, too." He walked over and hugged her, kissing her forehead. It took everything in her to hold her tongue, to stop herself from beating at his chest and asking him why. Why, after all she had shared with him, after all they had been through, would he do this to her? Was he really that heartless? That cold? Or maybe this was his twisted interpretation of what he thought love was supposed to be.

She closed her eyes, concentrated on not falling apart. Loving him and hating him all at once.

He looked down at her, cradling her face in his hands, "The party has taken on a life of its own. I doubt anyone would miss us if we left."

Thank God, because she wasn't sure how much more of this she could take. It wasn't supposed to be like this.

"How about we say our goodbyes and go home?"

Home. That word had taken on a whole new meaning in the past fifteen minutes, but she smiled and said, "Let's go."

They made the rounds, her cheeks aching from forced smiles. There was nothing about it that didn't completely suck. Emotionally, she was barely hanging by a thread when they finally made it to the car. Just fifteen more minutes she told herself as he started the engine, then they would be at the apartment where she could unravel in private. Decide what she was going to do with the rest of her life.

She'd never felt so sad. So utterly and completely alone.

Arching against the dull ache in her back, she turned her head to the window, rolled it down so she could feel the warm air on her cheeks, to dry the tears that had started falling.

It wasn't fair. But life never was. Not for her.

He dropped her at the door and she went upstairs while he parked. For a brief moment she caught herself thinking how nice it was going to be to have a garage. Would she? What would happen now? Divorce? Annulment?

She stepped into the apartment. They'd left the light on in the kitchen—they always forgot that one—and the lamp beside the sofa was lit. She looked around at his things and her things all mixed in together, like they belonged that way. It felt like home. But it was all an illusion.

She set her backpack down, and armed with a box of tissue, locked herself in the bathroom, giving herself permission to let go and sob her heart out. But of course the tears refused to come. Maybe she was so broken, she was numb.

Giving up, she walked to the bedroom and flopped down on the bed in the dark. Now what? Pack a bag? Wait it out?

She heard Tony come in, the jingle of his keys as he dropped them on the table, where he would inevitably lay the newspaper, or forms from the contractor. Which would instigate a search for said keys, and Lucy would usually find them before he did. It was almost a routine.

Was she just supposed to forget that?

"Still awake?" Tony asked upon seeing her sprawled out. Probably looking a bit like a beached whale. One with stretch marks and fat ankles.

She felt like she could close her eyes and sleep for a month, and at the same time she felt as if she would never sleep again. He had turned her entire world upside down.

"I'm awake," she said.

He switched on the light by the bed. "It's too bad we can't fool around."

"The doctor said not in my last month. You wouldn't want to prematurely induce my labor, would you?" She shifted, trying to get comfortable. Her back was really killing her now. She'd been fanatical about not taking any sort of pain reliever while she was pregnant, but she might have to break down and take an aspirin.

"You look uncomfortable," he said.

"Of course I'm uncomfortable," she snapped. "I'm

eight and a half months pregnant, as big as a house, my feet look like balloons and my back is killing me."

He winced, as if he could feel her pain. "Maybe you could try rolling on your side and hugging a pillow."

She wished he would stop being so nice. He seemed so sincere. So concerned. And damn it, it did feel better when she rolled on her side.

She couldn't do this anymore. Not with her heart breaking. She had to say something.

He walked to the bathroom, and a minute later she heard him brushing his teeth.

Do it, Lucy. Be brave.

"So I guess Rose kinda hit the nail on the head about this family having secrets, huh?" she called to him.

She heard him mumble something incoherent.

"Because everyone has secrets," she said. "Even you."

He poked his head out the bathroom door and grinned, toothpaste on his chin, looking so adorable she wanted to punch him. "My life is an open book."

With pages missing. Big pages.

Time to fill in the blanks.

"Are you sure about that?"

She heard him put his toothbrush away, and knew he was wiping his chin on the towel hanging beside the sink. He would shove it back in the ring haphazardly, backward so the stripes were on the wrong side. She knew his routine like the back of her hand.

He walked out of the bathroom wearing only a pair of boxers. "Nothing is coming to mind."

"Think harder."

He sat on the mattress beside her, stroked her belly. "Lucy, what's wrong? Did something happen at the party? Did someone say something that hurt your feelings?"

Rather than throw Carrie under the bus, since she was

only supporting her best friend, Lucy said, "Thirty million dollars. Now, that is a *sweet* deal."

Tony dropped his head and mumbled a curse. He knew he was busted. "Who told you?"

"It doesn't matter."

"Lucy—"

"I don't even know what to say to you."

"You need to know that it's not about the money. It was *never* about the money."

"I'm just supposed to take your word for it?"

"Well," he said calmly, as if this whole thing was just some silly understanding. "I would have hoped that by now you would trust me, but if you need definitive proof, I have it."

Fourteen

This should be good, Lucy thought. "So prove it."

"I can't. Not yet."

How stupid did she look? "Not yet? What is that supposed to mean?"

"I can prove to you that I am telling you the truth. I just can't do it right now."

That was the dumbest thing she'd ever heard. With effort she sat up. "Why not?"

"I'm already in the doghouse. If I break a promise now, I'll never live it down."

"A promise to *Nonno*," she said, the empty space in her soul growing larger by the minute. Trumped by *family* once again.

"No. Not *Nonno*."

"That surprised her a little. "If not *Nonno*, then who?"

"I can't tell you that."

"Why not?"

"The act of telling you who I made the promise to would in itself be breaking the promise. Does that make sense?"

"None at all. You realize that our marriage is on the line here."

"I do. I still can't say."

What was she missing? Who would Tony be so loyal to that he would put his marriage in jeopardy? And what could he possibly say that would prove he wasn't interested in the money.

"Think about it," he said. "The act of telling you who I made the promise to would in itself be breaking the promise."

He was getting at something, but she had no idea what. "You're going to have to give me more than that."

He shrugged. "I can't."

She concentrated, trying to clear her head, determined to figure this out. Who would he have made a promise to? And what did it have to do with him being in the doghouse. What could he say to her to prove it wasn't about the money?

Something clicked, and she gasped, then a laugh burst from chest. "Oh, my God. We're having a girl."

Tony's smile said it all.

A little girl.

And he knew all this time.

He pulled her into his arms and held her. What was she was always saying about giving people the benefit of the doubt? Instead she had rushed to a conclusion and made herself miserable for no reason at all.

After all they had been through, she should have trusted him.

"I'm such an idiot," she said.

"No, I should have told you about the money," he said. "But I made a promise to *Nonno*—"

"And your family always comes first. Yeah, I know."

He cupped her face. "No. You come first. You and

the baby. *Always*." He pressed a kiss to her lips. "I love you, Lucy."

"You could have told me. You can trust me."

"I screwed up. I didn't want to be *that* guy."

"What guy?"

"The one who deep down knows he doesn't deserve the woman he loves, and figures that if he tells her the truth, she would never forgive him his profane stupidity."

Forgive him? It was what she loved most about him.

He pressed a kiss to the top of her hand. "Lucy, I was a mess when you left. And yes, I made some pretty lousy decisions, like not telling you the truth immediately. I screwed up. And I'll screw up again, because apparently, that's who I am."

She could live with that.

"There's something that's been bugging me," he said. "How did you know that I was getting married to Alice. Who told you?"

"A friend."

"Who?"

"The email was signed, 'from a friend.' I didn't recognize the address."

Tony laughed. "Are you saying that you don't know who sent it?"

She bit her lip and shook her head.

"That was some leap of faith on your part."

Or sheer stupidity. Either way, everything turned out like it was supposed to.

She wrapped her arms around him, holding on tight. "I'm sorry I didn't trust you. It won't happen again."

"No, it probably will. Because that's who *you* are."

She hated to admit it, but he was right. It was in her

nature not to trust people. It was etched deep in her soul. "I'm sorry. I'm trying."

He touched her face. "Hey, it'll take time, but we'll get there. Both of us. It's not supposed to be easy. Right?"

No, it wasn't, and presently, they were only making it harder on themselves. "From now on, if there's a problem, we come to each other first. I don't care what it is."

"Agreed," he said.

Her back throbbed and she arched against the pain.

"Lay down," he said. "I'll rub your back."

She curled onto her side around a pillow.

"Is it your sciatic nerve acting up again?" he asked, gently kneading the muscles, and after a minute they began to loosen and uncoil.

"That's a sharp, intense pain, like a hot poker in my butt cheek. This is a dull ache. Like a spasm."

"So it's a spasm that comes and goes?"

She looked at him over her shoulder. "Isn't that what makes it a spasm? The coming and going?"

"How often have you been getting these spasms?"

"I'm not sure. I wasn't really keeping track."

"Maybe we should."

"It's just a backache."

"Are you sure?"

"Labor is sharp and intense, and in the front. What I feel now is more like a dull ache across my lower back."

"I remember my cousin Jessica saying that she had back labor with her kids."

"It's too early."

"You're thirty-eight weeks. That's considered full term."

"Tony, I am not in labor. I'm not ready."

"I don't think it works that way."

Jeez, would he give it a rest. "Less talking, more rubbing," she said.

"Like I haven't heard that before," he teased.

She smiled and closed her eyes. When she opened them again, the room was dark, and Tony lay wrapped around her, sound asleep.

Tony slept like the dead. He woke sometime around three-thirty, and when he reached for Lucy the mattress beside him was warm, but empty. Assuming she was in the bathroom, he drifted back to sleep. He woke several hours later, as the initial, pinkish glow of dawn leaked through the partially open blinds, and discovered he was alone again. Only this time her side was cold.

How long had she been up?

Rubbing the sleep from his eyes he rolled out of bed and tugged on a pair of jeans and went looking for her. She was in the kitchen sipping a cup of tea and pacing.

She looked exhausted.

"Good morning," he said, and she stopped moving only long enough to kiss him. "Back still hurting?"

"It's driving me crazy," she said wearily. "I think you may be right."

"You think it's labor?"

"That or kidney stones. I tried timing the pains, but they're all over the place. Two minutes, then fifteen."

"How long have you been up?"

"A couple of hours," she said, looking tired and miserable. "But even when I was in bed, I couldn't sleep. Every time I doze off, it starts to hurt again."

"You should have woken me up."

"There wasn't much you could do. And you need your sleep. If this is labor it's probably going to be a long day. And at least she waited until after we were married."

He could have at least kept her company. "Come here. Lean forward and rest your elbows on the counter."

"Hey!" she said when he lifted her nightshirt up. "What do you think you're doing back there?" He started rubbing her lower back and she collapsed in an exhausted heap against the cool marble. "On second thought, I don't care, just keep doing it. That feels heavenly."

He rubbed gently, feeling the muscles tighten under his fingers as another contraction started. That one passed, and only a few minutes later another started. They kept up like that for a good forty-five minutes, and according to the stopwatch on his cell phone, occurred every twelve to fifteen minutes. The doctor had told them that with a first baby not to come in until the contractions were a steady five minutes apart. He'd also warned them that first labors could last for days.

"Is there anything I can do for you?" he asked Lucy, wishing he could make the pain disappear. Make her stop hurting.

"You could call the hospital," she said, wincing against another contraction, her breathing slow and shallow. "Tell them we'll be there soon."

"It could still be a while," he said.

"I don't think so. Either my bladder just gave out, or my water just broke."

When they got to the hospital, Lucy was dilated to only two centimeters. And after three hours of pacing the delivery ward, Tony and his mom taking turns walking with her, she'd progressed to only three centimeters.

The nurse gave her an injection to speed things up, and instantly the contractions went from six minutes apart to two minutes and according to the monitor they had strapped her to, almost doubled in intensity. Up until that point she had refused an epidural, or any sort of pain medication. Three contractions later, she was begging for anything to take the edge off.

It was an all-new ball game now. He was excited and scared and anxious. But mostly he was proud of Lucy. If she hadn't been his hero before, she sure would be now. As far as he was concerned, any woman who gave birth deserved a medal. He had seen a show some time ago about a man who, through the use of small electrical nodes, was able to accurately recreate the pain of labor. He used the method on himself, to prove that men had the same, if not a higher threshold for pain than women.

He lasted three hours, and then had to give up.

Men, Tony believed, were inherently wusses, but they were also ridiculously prideful. He didn't doubt that when it came to pain, Lucy had a will of steel.

"I hope she's going to be happy as an only child," Lucy said coming down off a particularly hard contraction. "Because there is no way in *hell* I'm doing this again."

"Every new mom says that," Sarah told her, swabbing her forehead with a cool rag. Lucy's hair was soaked with sweat and sticking to her forehead. "But everyone forgets."

Tony kissed her forehead, smoothed back her damp hair. "Lucy, you are doing an amazing job. I'm so proud of you."

"I just want the pain to stop," she said, looking tired and miserable.

"It will," he promised. "Just hang on a little while longer."

Several contractions later, when the nurse came in to check Lucy's progress, Lucy begged her for an epidural. She had been a real trouper up to that point, but Tony could see that she was exhausted.

"Let's check your progress first." She checked Lucy's cervix, which looked so uncomfortable it made him cringe. "Breathe through it, honey," the nurse said.

When she was done, Lucy pleaded, "Can I have drugs now?"

"Sorry, hon, but you're fully dilated. It's time to get ready to push."

Fifteen

The baby weighed in at a respectable seven pounds two ounces, and was born with a shock of long, jet-black hair. She had Lucy's eyes and Tony's nose.

Oh, and she had a penis.

"I still don't believe it," Tony said from the rocking chair beside her bed, where he cradled their sleeping son. Far as she could tell, he hadn't stopped chuckling since the doctor called out, "It's a boy!"

"I definitely saw girl parts on that ultrasound," Tony had insisted, while the doctor assured him that he definitely had not. Because despite popular belief, human fetuses did not spontaneously change gender.

"I guess it was a good thing you didn't tell me," Lucy said. "Or I fear our son would be wearing a lot of pink."

"You realize that if Rob and Nick don't have a son someday, this little guy will single-handedly have to carry on the Caroselli name."

"Only if he wants to," Lucy said. "Our son is going to be exactly who he wants to be. Nothing more, nothing less."

Tony's mom had been with them for the birth and

shortly after, Tony's dad joined them, beaming at his third grandchild. The flowers—and the visitors—started to pour in a steady stream after that until the room was filled to capacity. Someone passed around chocolate cigars, and everyone sipped on sparkling cider. They were loud and nosy and all-around nuts, but she loved them. They had sucked her in, made her part of the family, just as Tony said they would. She was one of them now.

Rob showed up alone, and after a quick peek at the baby, who was sleeping in his father's arms, he sat on the side of the bed. "On behalf of my wife, I'd like to apologize to you, Lucy. It was terrible what she did."

Honestly, she was beginning to think Carrie had done her a favor. She forced Lucy to realize how important it was to trust Tony. "You don't have to apologize. Everything turned out okay."

"For what it's worth, she feels horrible. She's been having a rough go of it lately and she lashed out."

"We all make mistakes," she said.

It was shaping up to be another perfect day. Then *Nonno* showed up.

Though Lucy had every right to be angry with him, she was too happy, and too content to ruin this special day. Sadly, he would never be more to her than Tony's grandfather. But she could live with that. As long as she had Tony, and their son, she didn't need anyone else.

Gradually people cleared out until only Tony's parents and *Nonno* remained.

"I'd like a private word with my grandson," *Nonno* told Tony's parents.

They left to get dinner.

"I have something for you," *Nonno* said, turning to Tony. "In the pocket of my shirt."

Tony pulled out a folded slip of paper. "A check?"

Nonno nodded.

Tony unfolded it and his mouth fell open. "Oh my God, this is a check for ten million dollars."

"It is."

"I can't take this," he said, handing it back. "Absolutely not."

"It's your severance."

Tony blinked. "Severance for what?"

"Your loyal years at Caroselli Chocolate."

"Wait a minute. Are you saying I'm *fired?*"

"As of today."

"But—" Tony paused, shook his head and laughed. "How did you know I wanted out?"

"I make it my business to know. There's a reason I consider you the most loyal of my grandsons. And I know what's good for you."

Tony opened his mouth to argue—or so she assumed—but he laughed instead. "It was you, wasn't it? You were the 'friend'"—he made quotes with his fingers— "who sent Lucy the email. You told her to come here so I wouldn't marry Alice. Somehow you knew about Lucy. And the baby. Didn't you? You got us back together."

"You have a vivid imagination, Antonio."

"Actually, I've always considered myself fairly practical, like my grandfather. In fact, if I were to bribe my grandsons with thirty million dollars, I would probably assume that once they fell in love and married they would no longer want the money."

According to what Tony told Lucy, that was exactly what had happened. Had he planned this from the start? Was Tony implying that his grandfather never intended to give his grandsons the thirty million dollars?

"Young people," *Nonno* said, with a shake of his head

and a twinkle in his eye, but he wasn't fooling either one of them. And she and Tony both knew that he wouldn't cop to it in a million years.

Shortly after that *Nonno* complained of being tired, so Tony walked him down to the car. When he came back, he cuddled with Lucy and the baby on the bed.

This is it, she thought, this was what it felt like to be truly happy.

"You know," Tony said, "I always resented that *Nonno* felt it was his place to tell everyone how to live, but look how happy we are. Rob and Nick are, too. I guess he knew what was best for everyone after all."

"I don't care what he knows or doesn't know. All that matters is that we're together," she said.

"You know the scariest part about this? At ninety-two years old, he orchestrated this entire production, and in the end he got exactly what he wanted."

"He did," she agreed, "but I think you're missing the point."

"What point?"

She smiled and kissed him. "So did we."

* * * * *

*If you liked Tony and Lucy's story,
pick up the other books in
The Caroselli Inheritance trilogy
from* USA TODAY *bestselling author
Michelle Celmer.*

CAROSELLI'S CHRISTMAS BABY
CAROSELLI'S BABY CHASE

All available now from Harlequin Desire!

#2305 MY FAIR BILLIONAIRE
by Elizabeth Bevarly
To land his biggest deal, self-made billionaire Peyton needs to convince
high society he's one of them. With help from Ava, his old nemesis, Peyton
transforms himself, but is it him or his makeover that captures Ava's heart?

#2306 EXPECTING THE CEO'S CHILD
Dynasties: The Lassiters • by Yvonne Lindsay
When celeb CEO Dylan Lassiter learns Jenny's pregnant after their one
night together, he proposes. To keep her past a secret, media-shy Jenny
refuses him. But Dylan will only accept "I do" for an answer!

#2307 BABY FOR KEEPS
Billionaires and Babies • by Janice Maynard
Wealthy Dylan Kavanagh loves being a hero, so when single mom Mia
needs help, Dylan offers her a room—at his place. But close proximity soon
has Dylan thinking about making this little family his—for keeps.

#2308 THE TEXAN'S FORBIDDEN FIANCÉE
Lone Star Legends • by Sara Orwig
Jake and Madison once loved each other, until their families' feud tore
them apart. Now, years later, the sexy rancher is back, wanting Madison's
oil-rich ranch—and the possibility of a second chance!

#2309 A BRIDE FOR THE BLACK SHEEP BROTHER
At Cain's Command • by Emily McKay
To succeed in business, Cooper Larson strikes a deal with his former
sister-in-law, the perfect society woman. When sparks fly, they're both
shocked, but Cooper will have to risk everything to prove it's her and not
her status he covets.

#2310 A SINFUL SEDUCTION
by Elizabeth Lane
When wealthy philanthropist Cal Jeffords tracks down the woman he
believes embezzled millions from his foundation, he only wants the
missing money. Then he wants her. But can he trust her innocence?

REQUEST YOUR FREE BOOKS!
2 FREE NOVELS PLUS 2 FREE GIFTS!

HARLEQUIN®

Desire

ALWAYS POWERFUL, PASSIONATE AND PROVOCATIVE

YES! Please send me 2 FREE Harlequin Desire® novels and my 2 FREE gifts (gifts are worth about $10). After receiving them, if I don't wish to receive any more books, I can return the shipping statement marked "cancel." If I don't cancel, I will receive 6 brand-new novels every month and be billed just $4.55 per book in the U.S. or $4.99 per book in Canada. That's a savings of at least 13% off the cover price! It's quite a bargain! Shipping and handling is just 50¢ per book in the U.S. and 75¢ per book in Canada.* I understand that accepting the 2 free books and gifts places me under no obligation to buy anything. I can always return a shipment and cancel at any time. Even if I never buy another book, the two free books and gifts are mine to keep forever.

225/326 HDN F4ZC

Name _____ (PLEASE PRINT)

Address _____ Apt. #

City _____ State/Prov. _____ Zip/Postal Code

Signature (if under 18, a parent or guardian must sign)

Mail to the **Harlequin® Reader Service:**
IN U.S.A.: P.O. Box 1867, Buffalo, NY 14240-1867
IN CANADA: P.O. Box 609, Fort Erie, Ontario L2A 5X3

Want to try two free books from another line?
Call 1-800-873-8635 or visit www.ReaderService.com.

* Terms and prices subject to change without notice. Prices do not include applicable taxes. Sales tax applicable in N.Y. Canadian residents will be charged applicable taxes. Offer not valid in Quebec. This offer is limited to one order per household. Not valid for current subscribers to Harlequin Desire books. All orders subject to credit approval. Credit or debit balances in a customer's account(s) may be offset by any other outstanding balance owed by or to the customer. Please allow 4 to 6 weeks for delivery. Offer available while quantities last.

Your Privacy—The Harlequin® Reader Service is committed to protecting your privacy. Our Privacy Policy is available online at www.ReaderService.com or upon request from the Harlequin Reader Service.

We make a portion of our mailing list available to reputable third parties that offer products we believe may interest you. If you prefer that we not exchange your name with third parties, or if you wish to clarify or modify your communication preferences, please visit us at www.ReaderService.com/consumerchoice or write to us at Harlequin Reader Service Preference Service, P.O. Box 9062, Buffalo, NY 14269. Include your complete name and address.

HD13R

The sound of the door buzzer alerted Jenna to a customer
out front. She pasted a smile on her face and walked out
into the showroom only to feel the smile freeze in place
as she recognized Dylan Lassiter, in all his decadent glory,
standing with his back to her, his attention apparently
captured by the ready-made bouquets she kept in the
refrigerated unit along one wall.

Her reaction was instantaneous—heat, desire and shock
each flooded her in turn. The last time she'd seen him had been
in the coat closet where they'd impulsively sought refuge,
releasing the sexual energy that had ignited so dangerously
and suddenly between them.

"Can I help you?" she asked, feigning a lack of recognition
right up until the moment he turned around and impaled her
with those cerulean-blue eyes of his.

Her mouth dried. It was a crime against nature that any
man could look so beautiful and so masculine all at the same
time.

A hank of softly curling hair fell across his high forehead,
making her hand itch to smooth it back, to then trace the
stubbled line of his jaw.

She'd spent the past two and a half months in a state of disbelief at her actions. It had literally been a one-night *stand*, she reminded herself cynically. The coat closet hadn't allowed for anything else. Her body still remembered every second of how he'd made her feel—and reacted in kind again.

"Jenna," Dylan acknowledged with a slow nod of his head, his gaze not moving from her face for a second.

"Dylan," she said, feigning surprise. "What brings you back to Cheyenne?"

The instant she said the words she silently groaned. Of course he was here for the opening of his new restaurant. The local chamber of commerce—heck, the whole town—was abuzz with the news. She'd tried to ignore anything Lassiter-related for weeks now, but there was no ignoring the man in front of her.

The father of her unborn child.

Don't miss EXPECTING THE CEO'S CHILD
by Yvonne Lindsay, available June 2014.

Wherever Harlequin® Desire
books and ebooks are sold.

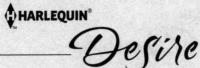

ALWAYS POWERFUL, PASSIONATE AND PROVOCATIVE.

BABY FOR KEEPS
Billionaires and Babies
by **Janice Maynard**

"I have a proposition for you."

Wealthy Dylan Kavanagh loves being a hero, so when single
mom Mia needs help, Dylan offers her a room—at his place.
But close proximity soon has Dylan thinking about making
this little family his—for keeps.

Look for
BABY FOR KEEPS
in June 2014, from Harlequin® Desire!
Wherever books and ebooks are sold.

Don't miss other scandalous titles from the
Billionaires and Babies miniseries,
available now wherever books and ebooks are sold.

Billionaires and Babies: Powerful men…wrapped around their
babies' little fingers

HD73320

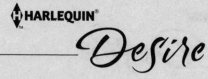

HARLEQUIN®

Desire

ALWAYS POWERFUL, PASSIONATE AND PROVOCATIVE.

A BRIDE FOR THE BLACK SHEEP BROTHER

At Cain's Command
by Emily McKay

"I don't think I'm the right woman for you."

To succeed in business, Cooper Larson strikes a deal with his former sister-in-law, the perfect society woman. Cooper's hunger for his former sister-in-law hasn't abated over the years. When sparks fly, they're both shocked, but Cooper will have to risk everything to prove it's her and not her status he covets.

Look for
A BRIDE FOR THE BLACK SHEEP BROTHER
in June 2014, from Harlequin® Desire!

Wherever books and ebooks are sold.

Don't miss other exciting titles from the
At Cain's Command miniseries by Emily McKay,
available now wherever ebooks are sold.

ALL HE REALLY NEEDS

ALL HE EVER WANTED

HD73322